About *The Celestials*

'*The Celestials is a marvel – radical and contemplative, adventurous and moving.*' Barry Hill, poet and historian

'*The Celestials is profound meditation on the quality of human pilgrimage through the landscapes of China and Australia. An epic and rich narrative. Vitality, power, pathos and keenly humane observation, resonances which touch and elucidate the world of contemporary Australia.*' Richard Mills AM, composer and Artistic Director, Victorian Opera

'*The Celestials is a love song to this country. As a Eurasian woman I was deeply moved.*' Vanessa Maria Bates, playwright

'*Writing of heart-felt delicacy miraculously turns one of Australia's best-known episodes on its head with radical reimagining, yet drawn from intriguing research of the historical record. The Celestials is a revelation in its stillness as it recounts well-known events of outrageous violence and rebellion.*' Jonathan Mills, composer and director of festivals in Edinburgh and Melbourne

'*Life on the New Gold Mountain is depicted in The Celestials in all its complexity, its ugliness and beauty, from perspectives that have almost been forgotten by Australian history.*' Hoa Pham, Playwright, Author of *The Other Shore*.

The
Celestials
Ian David Roberts

MELBOURNE & GALWAY

© 2023 Ian David Roberts

First published 2023 by ARDEN
the general books' imprint of
Australian Scholarly Publishing Pty Ltd
7 Lt Lothian St Nth, North Melbourne, Vic 3051

Tel: 03 9329 6963
enquiry@scholarly.info / www.scholarly.info

ISBN 978-1-922952-80-6 (hardback)

ALL RIGHTS RESERVED

Cover design: Lucia Sankovic
Images: Ian David Roberts

This book is dedicated to my wife, Jane Peart,
and to my teacher, Thich Nhat Hanh.

Contents

Preface	ix
Prologue	1
The War Goes On and On	4
The Other Shore	38
Proceeding Namelessly	47
Little Wattles Love Raw Ground	70
Longing That Cannot Be Separated	90
Mayday	112
The Mirror Itself	164
Timeline of Historic Events	211
The Heart Sutra	218
Acknowledgements	226

Preface

This story is a fiction which winds its way through some well-known facts and some lesser-known matters on the public record.

The two main characters and the lives they lead are my invention. Their interaction with real people and real events has been inspired by the sources listed at the back of this book.

In my view, it is entirely possible that what unfolds within these pages could have happened. It is such a shame no one took a deeper interest in some of these lives, customs, histories and relationships at the time.

As one of the fictitious characters says, 'there are too many untold stories around this place'.

Finally, I acknowledge that the Chinese language spoken at the time of this story in the Colony of Victoria was Cantonese. However, on the advice of Chinese colleagues, Mandarin characters and pinyin are used for the benefit of a wider readership.

Ian David Roberts 2023

*My actions are my only true belongings. I cannot
escape the consequences of my actions.
My actions are the ground on which I stand.*
Thich Nhat Hanh

Prologue

During the eighteenth century, the British people's love of Chinese silk, porcelain, jade carvings, pearl-inlaid furniture and teas of the most remarkable and fragrant kinds, pushed the United Kingdom into an ever-increasing trade debt with China. The British Government was determined to reverse this trade deficit. To do so they needed to find a product which they could control, and which the Chinese simply had to have.

The British found what they wanted in India. It was opium and, with full knowledge of its addictive qualities, they set about turning the people of China into addicts. By the 1830s their efforts were so successful that the Qing Dynasty attempted to ban opium and, to that end, the Emperor even sought help from Queen Victoria to whom in mid-1839, his viceroy, Lin Zexu, wrote:

> *We have heard in your own country [that] opium is prohibited with the utmost strictness ... This is strong proof that you know full well how hurtful it is to mankind. Since you do not permit it to injure your own country, you ought not have the injurious drug transferred to another.*

A year later, when no support was forthcoming from the British Crown, Commissioner Lin seized stockpiles of the drug. In response, on 4 September 1839, the British declared war on China. That act of unprovoked aggression became known as the First Opium War. It marked the beginning of what the Chinese call *bainian guochi* 百年国耻, The Hundred Years of National Humiliation. The ongoing sense of humiliation which they endured in that century did not just afflict those who lived within the broken-down gates of the Celestial Kingdom. It followed them wherever they went.

'Old Canton' map based on the cartography of the Reverend Daniel Vrooman, an American missionary to China in 1866. He later became the superintendent of a 'Mission to the Chinese' in Victoria, Australia, in 1878.

The War Goes On and On

*This same moon shines
where I grew up.
My brothers are scattered
no way to know if they are alive.*

(Du Fu Tang Dynasty Poet)

Li Ping was sixteen years old and her brother Li Chen was nineteen.

Li Chen knew the back streets of Guangzhou and the area around Kun Yam Hill well. Each day he walked the length of the inner walled city, passing through the south gate into the outer wall precinct and then on to the street of the jade stone factories and workshops. It was here he learned his trade as a jade stone carver beside the Zhujiang River 珠江, making amulets for the merchant guild, the *Cohong*. The Qing Emperor authorised the guild to deal with the British East India Company.

Li Chen's favorite amulet was the white jade comb with two cranes carved into the stock – a symbol of the bond between father and son. But the amulets began to have another meaning for Li Chen. Perhaps not even a meaning, more a feeling he never tried to put into words. When he imagined an English woman plying it through her fair hair for the first time, he felt his breath quicken.

Li Chen's turning from youth to man excited him but concerned his parents and his sister. He had become a clever card player and spent many nights at card games behind the factories and tea houses and, almost certainly, in opium rooms. He would often take his moon-shaped string instrument, *the yueqin* 月琴, with him and loved to play the old tunes, especially those about marching armies and horsemen. At home, he played slow melodies about the moon and he loved his sister closing her eyes to listen.

Li Chen and Li Ping's father, Li Wencui was a clever, educated man who achieved high marks in the *keju* 科举, the Imperial Examinations.

Working as an actuary for one of the merchant guilds, Li Wencui knew the value of education. The one gift he was intent on bestowing upon his family was literacy and he spent much of his income hiring private tutors.

Yet, for all his apparent success, Li Wencui wondered how he had lost his youthful rebellious spirit. In these moments of disappointment with himself, he recalled his favourite book as a student, *The Unofficial History of the Scholars*. He remembered the delight and optimism he had felt when the author, Wu Jingsi, honoured Confucius and mocked the self-righteous academics.

However, in these times as a husband and father

he wished that he could be a braver man. His lack of courage sickened him.

Li Ping accepted the gift of private education with great dedication and learned quickly, though Li Chen did not respond so well to intellectual nourishment. When his son entered his teens, Li Wencui was sick with fear that Li Chen would take up opium, the drug introduced by the British which had robbed the country of its vitality, its *qi* 气 – energy – for decades.

Entire territories, including Hong Kong, were ceded to England after its military conquered China's weak government to protect its opium trade. Untold millions of pounds were made by the British East India Company and myriad dealers driving millions of people into the abyss of addiction.

Li Ping's mother, Cai Yinhong, was born of a long line of herbalists and pharmacists. The deep knowledge acquired through more generations than Cai Yinhong could number, was passed down through the males of the family. Their apothecaries were known for the potency of their herbs and their skilfully balanced preparations.

As a young girl, Cai Yinhong spent many hours each week helping her father in the family's wood and stone shop, sorting fresh herbs into the drying racks. She stocked the drawers of her great-grandfather's apothecary cabinet with forensically cleaned and sorted seeds, petals, leaves, roots, stamens, kernels and skins of both animal and vegetable.

When she was very young, the great cabinet towered over her, like a temple she thought, and she would stand on his old stool to refill the highest drawers. She loved how the order and care taken in the pungent little shop could heal so many injuries and sicknesses. Here, in my hands, she thought, is the salve of nature.

Cai Yinhong's dedication to the little shop was noticed by everyone. It seemed that she always knew the value of her service, even though, as a female only child, she would never be fully educated in the profession she loved. And she would never inherit the goods and chattels or the financial advantage of the ageless enterprise. She would never inherit a home.

Nevertheless, she continued her service till the day of her arranged marriage to Li Wencui, a kind but uncertain man. After the arrival of their first-born, he welcomed her request to work at an apothecary recently opened for business just a few streets away from her new family home.

One evening, in the season of the mangosteens and only a month after their marriage, Li Wencui sat beside his young wife with a book in his hands. They had just finished their evening meal of *lo foh tong* 老火湯 – Old Fire Soup. Li Wencui lit the oil lamp and, as he opened the book, said:

'Beloved wife, I would like to read you a book that

made a great impression on me when I was studying for the civil service examinations. It provides great amusement. It also tells us much about the decay which is occurring within our society and the corruption of the system of examinations.'

'Of course, husband. I will listen to every word, but I don't understand. You passed the examinations well and you have attained a modest position that keeps us secure and hopeful.'

'Yes, my beloved, we are secure now. But hope is not easy to live with in these times. This book, *The Unofficial History of the Scholars*, explains my concerns. It does so with humour as well as some outrageous revelations.'

'So – we laugh and cry together. Is that your wish, husband?'

Li Wencui smiled lightly and began to read.

⌣

Over the following five evenings, Li Wencui read chapter after chapter of the great satire. It was so biting at times, Cai Yinhong almost hushed him for fear that their reading and laughter might be overheard. Initially, Cai Yinhong flinched at stories about manipulative officials in high office and the obsequious academics who would do anything for more power. But her heart was warmed by the affection of the writer for the lower classes and the timeless wisdom of the sages, especially Confucius.

Cai Yinhong was thrilled by tales in which women

like her made pleasure trips to the mountains with their husbands, drinking wine and reading books. She was dumbfounded to hear a story about how concubines should be outlawed, and young women saved from humiliation.

The stories were exciting, and their critical content made her head and heart spin as she apprehended an entirely new world, a world so radical as to question her own beliefs.

'Husband, do you imagine that our life together might break so many traditions? What type of society do you think our children will join?'

Li Wencui put the book down and looked toward the ceiling timbers. Nervous, his first thought was to reassure his wife not to worry. He considered a reply, 'The book is just a book. An amusement with a sting in the tail.' But he knew it wasn't true. He knew the book was based on real people and real incidents occurring throughout the Celestial Kingdom every day.

Turning to his wife, he replied.

'I believe the book speaks the truth. I believe great change is inevitable. I believe our children need to live different lives. And I know it will require great strength to lead our family into this changing society.'

Cai Yinhong looked toward her husband, searching him closely, feeling his discomfort. And then a most unwanted thought crossed her mind. Perhaps he feels he has failed me already?

Cai Yinhong's work at the apothecary continued during her children's adolescence. She worried about opium, about how it had reduced so many children they knew to terrible dependence. And, what of her children? Most days at nightfall, just before she finished work and lit her lamp to walk home, Cai Yinhong would gather green herbs to make a tea which the doctor said would stave off the effects of the cursed *yapian* 鸦片 – opium. She prayed to the Bodhisattva Guanyin 观音 on every out-breath as she stepped from stone to stone – perhaps seven thousand steps in all.

Li Ping, a very studious young woman who loved literature, especially the writings of the sages, attended the Buddhist nunnery a few streets away almost every day. The nuns welcomed her to afternoon meditation and chanting. Afterwards, Li Ping loved to sit in silence surrounded by a blessing of women sipping tea. It was here that she first learned to chant the Heart Sutra. The swelling of the voices in unison lifted her, though the struggle to understand the bewildering ancient text embarrassed and annoyed her. Something akin to shame.

'Early days', whispered the monastic next to her.

On weekends and on special days of the lunar calendar, she went to the great Hualin Temple of the Five Hundred Genii, *Huallinsi wubailuohan* 华林寺五百罗汉. The corridors, antechambers and worship halls took her breath away. She walked softly in her silk temple slippers and, on sunny days, the reflected light from the gold figures coloured her hands as she pressed them together at the fingertips. She contemplated the great temple's first foundation stones being laid and then rising out of the ground more than a millennium before. The dharma talks by the Abbot about the arrival of the great Indian Buddhist missionary, Bodhidharma, who began the construction, made tears well, so intense was her feeling of undeserved kinship with the wise ones of the tradition. She felt unworthy in many ways yet was drawn to deepening her practice by whatever proper means.

There were many statues of Guanyin throughout the Temple of the Five Hundred Genii, but there was one unlike any other. On a late autumn morning, Li Ping slowed to a stop as she walked the hall where this Guanyin sat. She gazed on the unusual statue. The mythical deity was depicted with the right leg hitched up and the right bare foot planted solidly on a bench of stone. The right arm rested on the right knee, the left leg hanging easily over the edge of the bench, foot touching the ground. Loosely gathered robes spread out from the waist across opened legs.

Li Ping was caught by the torso – a beautiful, low-slung necklace dipping below the collarbone, its pendants lying on a lithe, half-exposed chest.

She had never seen a statue look so casual.

Sister Abbess noticed Li Ping's concentration. 'Guanyin sits in *rajalilasana*, a pose known as Royal Ease. Only a king or queen with an undefended heart, can sit in that way.'

Li Ping's gaze did not shift. 'But look at the chest and the wideness of the knees. And the confidence. Yet I feel confused. Is she male or female?'

'She is both, he is both. Li Ping, as you know, in the Heart Sutra we chant the name of the bodhisattva of compassion, or Saint of Mercy as the Jesuits say, as Avalokiteshvara. We recognise Avalokiteshvara, the

mystical being, as male. As Guanyin, the same bodhisattva is almost always manifested as female.'

The Abbess continued, 'Do you remember the words of the chant, "*no eye, no ear, no tongue, no mouth*"?'

'Yes, Sister', replied Li Ping.

'Well, my dear, I understand the words to mean that no individually identified object stands alone with a separate self.'

'Perhaps the sutra could include "no gender" as well.'

'There is no man without woman, no woman without man. The source and the essence of everything, however it is expressed or understood, is neither or both. I'm not equipped to solve a riddle like that. I simply content myself with feeling the bodhisattva as neither or both and that our most essential quality, compassion, must flow from both male and female. That's why sometimes he is she and sometimes she is he.'

'The teaching is that we should not be caught by names if we want to ease suffering. Gender is just another name.'

At home that night, Li Ping sat on the edge of her bed. Lifting her right foot on to the bed itself and resting her wrist on her knee, she allowed her left leg to hang casually over the edge of the bed. Her bare foot touched the floor.

She looked down on her slim chest, scarcely defined by breasts. Then she straightened her back, raised her head a little and smiled slightly as she felt her heart beat.

On Li Ping's next visit, Sister Abbess took her aside after chanting. She told Li Ping that she had noticed tightness in her voice during the Heart Sutra. The Abbess praised her dedication but said that Li Ping's mind was constricting her progress with the puzzling text. To overcome this, she was advised to travel beyond the city walls and

across the Zhujiang River to the Hoi Tong Monastery 海幢寺, named after the Indian monk Sagaradhvaja – a devout student of the Heart Sutra. 'There you will find Monastics so filled with the insight of the Sutra, you may be able to receive it without any thought at all.'

The Abbess added, 'I will accompany you – and your mother – if you wish'.

Li Ping was relieved by this offer. The forty-three lines of the text promised so much: eradication of all delusions, provision of deepest wisdom and, through that, entry to Nirvana. However, once the chant reached the phrase '*form is emptiness and emptiness is form*', Li Ping's mind churned in the search for a meaning. But before an answer arose, she found herself chanting '*no eye, nor ear, nor nose, nor tongue*'. Then something just gave up within her. By the time the sangha congregation reached the final phrase, she felt relief.

Gaté gaté pāragate pārasamgate bodhi svāhā.

Was it relief because it was over, or had the cryptic, paradoxical phrases begun to have their effect? Probably both, she thought, stretching her legs, readying to stand. Can this chanting penetrate me to the point that I fully see nothing is separate?

However, despite her questioning, her devotion to Guanyin, the great bodhisattva of compassion, grew as purposefully as any plant or vegetable. Sometimes, walking home, she smiled at the thought that there was a garden within her.

On the morning of the next full moon, Li Ping, her mother and Sister Abbess, walked south through the city past the offices of the Tartar in Chief of the Guangzhou Army Braves, past Governor Le's Palace, past the Protestant Chapel, through the southwest gate of the inner wall, past Li Chen's jade stone workshop, through the grounds of the Catholic Church and finally out the most southerly gate of the outer wall and into the gardens of the riverside Temple of Eternal Fragrances. There, on the water's edge, their boatman waited with his single oar hovering above the still waters of the Zhujiang River. Over his shoulder Li Ping saw the red and gold gates of the monastery for the first time. Her heart rose as she stepped aboard ready to commence the birthday celebrations of Guanyin. Everything around her seemed to be softening. Even the calls of the coots beneath the bow of the little boat seemed mere whisperings. Li Ping recalled the statue of Guanyin in the meditation hall at the nunnery – a beautiful young bodhisattva, neither fully male nor fully female, dressed in white robes and able to change forms to offer eternal mercy to all beings.

As they reached the landing outside the temple gates, the Great Bell began the call to meditation. Seven slow soundings rang out, each reaching into Li Ping's breastbone, with vibrations close to her heart. Clasping her mother's hand, she stepped along the path between the stands of ancient *baiyang* trees 白杨树 and the flags of many colours lining the walk to the Great Hall.

Ahead, robed monastics walked in slow procession like a single being – a golden caterpillar making its way back into its place of refuge. The lay community followed in respectful airy silence.

As Li Ping approached her cushion in the hall, she felt the air around her thicken with the breathing of the devoted congregation. She had never felt more willing to drop to her knees and let her forehead touch the oiled timber floor.

The Abbot Penshuang Xhia rang the temple bell three times, each ring spaced by three slow breaths. As one, the voice of the devoted congregation rose in the chant of the Heart Sutra.

For a time after the chant, Li Ping's mind cleared. Thought, feeling and body assumed the nature of water

– clear, formless. But as she reached out to grasp this clarity, it disappeared. All she could see were countless individual objects. All she could feel was struggle.

Sister Abbess leaned toward her and touched her loosely clasped hands. It was time to leave, but she wanted to remain and find herself as water again.

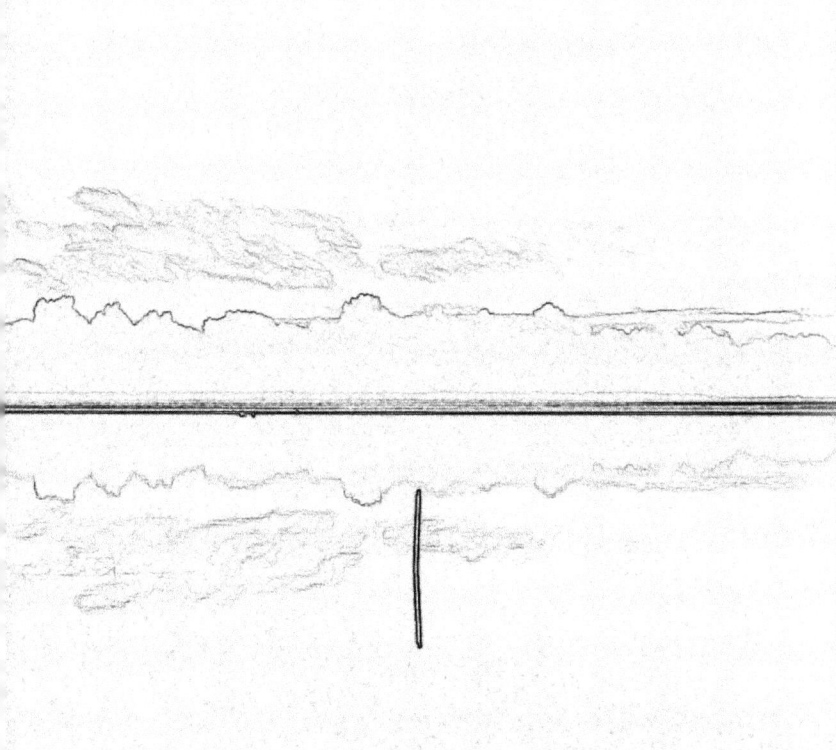

The monastics rose, bowed to the white marble Buddha and filed out toward the entrance portico. The lay congregation followed, Li Ping and her mother among them. When they reached the door, they stood together, turned and bowed once more towards the great teacher, a little more aware than before of their own Buddha nature. Outside, in the late morning sunshine, Sister Abbess led them through gardens lined with statues of the bodhisattvas and the many elegant earthen pots of rare miniature plants known as *penjing* 盆景. Beautifully rounded, fattening pigs brushed past their long, loose clothes roaming freely as though they knew that, within this devout community, they could live their lives to the full. Straight ahead lay the Kung Fu Hall where monks trained. It was not a place for women.

Sister Abbess took the southeast path through a bamboo forest so dense and tall that the little oil lanterns cast shadows over its long understorey grasses. They came to a clearing beyond which they could see the portico and sweeping roofline of the Great Library. Inside, between what seemed like hundreds of pagodas filled with books, Li Ping saw gold and silk-embroidered panels and scrolls depicting scenes of a breathtaking natural beauty that she had never seen before.

Foreign visitors, many of them Christian clerics and missionaries, came here on the eighth, eighteenth and twenty-eighth days of each month. The Abbot set those days aside for foreigners to immerse themselves in the ancient teachings. Li Ping felt proud that the great insights of the Buddha were available to foreigners. She was delighted that they had the opportunity to experience their beauty.

'Yes', said Sister Abbess, 'we must maintain our intention to share the teachings. Even when they are misunderstood.'

It saddened Li Ping deeply when Sister Abbess spoke about a Christian missionary, Reverend Bettelheim, who, after spending several days in the library, sharing tea and persimmons with the Abbot, wrote a condemnation of Buddhist practice in the English language journal, *The Chinese Repository*: '... *the people have been confirmed in their absurd superstitions and even led to suppose that Christians also derive some benefit from Budhistic [sic] witchcraft*'.

Sister Abbess continued, saying that Reverend Bettelheim and his wife had taken control of a small temple in a village outside Guangzhou. In the same issue of the journal, he also wrote,

> *How many hundreds are now at least practically prevented from idolatry, by the mere fact of our occupying this temple. Shall Buddhism rear again from its own ruins? Shall we restore a fort given up by the enemy? And now the enemy – Buddhistic priests*

and Confucian rulers – have surrendered his gods, shall we be forced into the foolish generosity of restoring them? Shall we let Satan loose after chaining him a little?

Li Ping was shocked. 'However', said Sister Abbess, 'not all foreigners seek to destroy our practice. The Jesuit Priests from the Catholic Church inside the city walls come here often. They call Guanyin the Goddess of Mercy. I only tell you this about the foreigners because there are more and more of them. They're still selling opium to our brothers and sisters whose addictions are never-ending. We need to be strong in our practice to help overcome this scourge.'

Li Ping understood what Sister Abbess meant. Her parents had often told her about the war with the British in 1841 – the year of her birth. While that conflict lay outside her experience, she understood the consequences of the British victory over her people. Opium addicts lay slumped in doorways throughout the city. The numbers of foreigners were increasing. European-controlled ships filled the wharves by the river and her parents frequently engaged in anxious, often hushed discussions with friends and neighbours about the failure of local and national authorities to protect the people.

The only time her parents' despair eased was when her father's anger overflowed. At such times, he would recount the fight at *Sanyuanli* 三元里, when thousands of

farmers and ordinary people rose up against the British garrison. The national government of the Celestial Kingdom not only capitulated to British demands that their opium-selling business continue but also agreed to pay compensation to the British and concede more Chinese cities like Hong Kong as trading ports for foreigners. 'Cowardice. Cowardice', Li Ping's father gasped. His humiliation was like annihilation.

Often, at the conclusion of such outbursts, Li Wencui would cover his face with his hands and weep, calling out the name of his son in some inarticulate plea. He was breaking down, fearful of his son becoming a victim of warfare and opium. Life was harder and harder to bear; the very foundation of their family was corroding.

But, still, as each day unfolded across the city, Li Ping remained steadfast. She walked to the nunnery, shopped with her mother at the market, admired Li Chen's latest jade carvings above the fireplace, made moon cakes for mid-Autumn Festival and listened to her father's evening readings of the Tang poets, especially, the master Du Fu:

New Moon

Such a thin moon
its first quarter
a slanting shadow
a partly finished ring
barely risen
over the ancient fort

hanging at the edge
of the evening clouds
the Milky Way
hasn't changed colour

the mountain passes
are cold and empty
there's white dew
in the front courtyard
secretly filling
the drenched carnations.

And so, life continued into her early teens until one evening, after dinner, her father turned to his beloved Du Fu and read a poem lamenting the loss of home and family. The last verse reads:

> *The letters we send each other*
> *Never seem to arrive*
> *And the war goes on and on.*

Li Ping's father had heard that the Governor's recent attempts to stop the opium trade had failed. The British fleet was on its way again to force submission and mass addiction on the Chinese people. 'The government has failed our people and I cannot protect my family.'

On the first day of the bombardment, Li Ping's parents took their children, and what food they could carry, to shelter in the nunnery at the end of their street. The smell of fires and pulverised stone seeped into the nuns' laundry where they took refuge. They held on to each other while lying between baskets of soiled robes and vestments. The Great Bell in the nunnery grounds sounded in strange, involuntary murmurs as the ground beneath it shook. Towards evening, nuns brought them bowls of rice water and then rushed away. Many more people arrived after their houses were gutted and fell in on themselves.

Hours turned to days and the family barely moved. When they came out of their shelter to see their street again, Li Ping realised that her sense of home had changed. The collapsed buildings had become places of a past life. The city's Museum, housing precious antiquities, had been bombed and then looted by the English in the guise of protecting Chinese cultural objects. She felt a powerful desire to return to the refuge of the nunnery.

Eventually, the bombing stopped. As soon as it was safe, Li Ping's father led the family to the Hualin Temple where he told them that he had raised sufficient money to

send them both to *Tsin Chin Shan* – New Gold Mountain – in distant New Holland, another British colony.

'The Heavenly Kingdom is living in two hells', he said. 'One created by the British and another by Hong Xiuquan 洪秀全 and his Taiping Rebellion armies which are killing thousands, perhaps millions of our own people to overthrow the cowardly Qing Dynasty. We may all be killed by the British or by our own people. Our society is being destroyed from within and without – there's nothing here for any of us anymore, particularly you, our children.'

~

He gave each of them three sticks of incense and, together, they went inside the great temple to pray for a safe passage and sufficient wealth to enable their return.

That evening, the homeless family returned to the refuge of the nunnery. Li Ping went directly to the library where she commenced learning poems and short sutras, word by word. They would stay with her, wherever she went for the rest of her life.

The hurried preparations for leaving unnerved Li Ping. Back at the nunnery, her father issued warnings about the dangers that they would face on the voyage and once they arrived in *Tsin Chin Shan*.

'There are many fast-flowing rivers to cross between Guangzhou and the ship awaiting you in Hong Kong harbour. Robbers prey on Chinese people trying to leave, while the emboldened foreign troops and traders will give you little respect and certainly no protection', he said.

He warned Li Ping and Li Chen that the sea voyage would take at least three months and maybe longer, depending on the winds. And he said, 'Chinese, American and English pirates are raiding ships out to sea from Hong Kong. I've heard through families whose men have returned, that the people in *Tsin Chin Shan* can be very rough.'

'They don't like us. Nor do the authorities there. But that's not a new condition for us to bear. The British control *Tsin Chin Shan* as well as our own city here.'

However, he also assured Li Ping and Li Chen of two factors in their favour: great fortunes were being made in the goldfields, and the number of people from Guangzhou in *Tsin Chin Shan* was great and growing.

'When you arrive in Melbourne town, you'll be met by members of the See Yup society who'll help you with everything you need including your banking. This is the advantage of travelling with a group, a *zhenying* 阵营, who are mostly from See Yup. There's a blacksmith, a gardener, a carpenter, four young farm labourers, a chef and two former soldiers who'll lead the *zhenying*. They've all been lent money by the same person I borrowed from – that's how I found them.'

'Finally,' he instructed, 'there's one very important matter you must never forget. You must come home with at least eight hundred Tael.'

Li Chen, who knew about ruthless money lenders' involvement in the opium trade, asked what would happen to their father if they couldn't get eight hundred Tael. 'What if we can't get anything? What if we can't return?'

'My son, I think you know the answer to those questions.'

Li Chen fell silent.

His father continued. 'Li Ping must stay close to you, Li Chen, always. She must live as a man for her own safety. It will not be easy here in our homeland or on the ship but, once you get to *Tsin Chin Shan*, the foreigners there will never know. They don't like to be close to us anyway.'

Li Ping was surprised but neither shocked nor sad. Her first thoughts were to turn her attention to Guanyin and prepare to leave the world of names and objects. She had been thinking about becoming a nun for some time, especially since taking refuge in the nunnery.

As preparations for their departure continued, Li Ping took her brother aside.

'Beloved Brother, I know what our father has said about me living as a man for my safety and I will do as he wishes. But I want you to know I do not feel this means of living will be a simple choice between appearing as male or female. I will live with you, my brother, as neither man nor woman – or *both* man and woman. It's very hard for me to explain and I'm sure I'll understand more as time passes, but the world of appearances and ornaments will never be a true indication of who I really am. Thank you, my brother, for being prepared to protect me in this way.'

Li Chen seemed perplexed, and Li Ping wondered if she had expressed what was emerging within her well enough.

⌣

Later in life, Li Ping would often recall the trip to Hong Kong and, with it, her final memories and images of her birth home. For the rest of her life, she enjoyed recalling the waterways of the Zhujiang Delta, and the birds nesting on the riverbanks. She loved to recall their flight above the sampans plying the river from shore to shore, like rows of ducks leaving little wakes for the others to follow, 'but the geese high above left no trace at all' she mused, recalling a poem from her childhood.

Li Ping came to see life as many deaths and many loves. She thought of her parents, their love for each other and their inevitable passing. For Li Ping, leaving the Celestial Kingdom was like a dying love. When she allowed herself to fall back into her memories of the Celestial Kingdom, she would often whisper to herself the love offering of the poet Yuan Hoawen.

Wild Geese

by Yuan Hoawen 元好问

I ask of the world, 'What is love' and why
love moves creatures to live or die?
To the north and to the south too
the pair of travellers are flying.
Many a winter and summer through,
the loving old couple have been winging.
But sorrow follows when the parting is done
For these soulmates also?
asks the surviving one.
I seem to hear the geese again.
Heavens may be jealous too.
Won't you believe?

And, soon after arriving on the southern continent, she confided some simple words to her notebook.

> *Winds and waves have brought us here, to this other shore. Can bird and ocean be my guide? How does the Curlew know the way across an undivided home?*

The Other Shore

Sister and brother left Hong Kong harbour on 17 January 1857 on the ship, the *Land O'Cakes*. The passenger manifest recorded the names of the thirty-one crew, including ten Chinese deck hands. It also included a scrawled notation, '*235 China passengers*'. Their individual names were not recorded; they were like animals being taken somewhere – 'livestock', as the British might say, or 'Merely Celestials', as the British crew called them.

Without names recorded, the Celestials became as untraceable as any bird or fish. They were cargo – an expensive cargo for the captain of the ship. If he took them to the Port of Melbourne, their paid destination, he would have to pay a special tax for each of them. The British colonial power which in China was turning Li Chen and Li Ping's people into opium addicts, did not welcome them as immigrants in the new Colony of Victoria. So, the captain of the *Land O'Cakes* put the Celestials into small boats off the coast near the town of Robe, in the Colony of South Australia, and had them rowed ashore. From there, they were left to walk to the goldfields hundreds of miles away.

Li Ping and Li Chen were two among thousands of Chinese gold-seekers filling the bilges and holds of trading ships. Just two more anonymous passengers abandoned on an ancient land recently invaded by the same empire whose greed was ruining their homeland. Their families in China would never know if Li Ping, Li Chen and their compatriots were lost at sea. They sailed on tickets bought with money borrowed from Chinese merchants dealing in opium supplied by the British – traitorous collaborators making easy profits from the promise of riches in the new British colony thousands of miles away to the south.

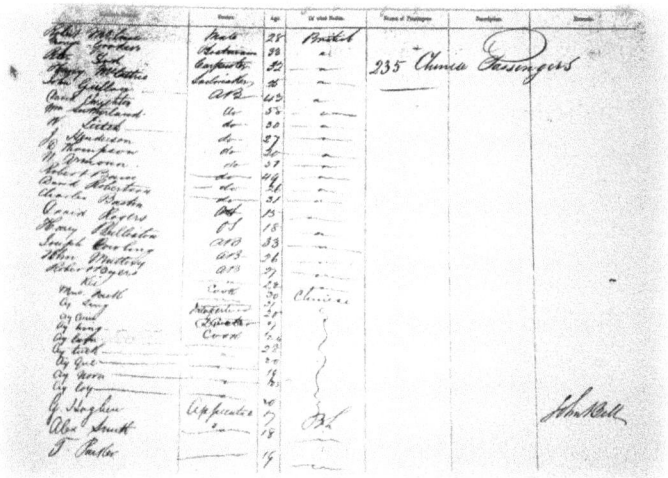

And, from the beginning, others who came the same way at the same time and for the same reasons despised the Celestials one and all. Even the convicts, who the British herded on to the island continent, had their names recorded. Their relatives will be able to find their details in colonial records forever. But those who might wish to find Li Ping, Li Chen and the two hundred and thirty-three others who travelled with them, will never find a thing.

~

Li Chen was a devoted brother and protected Li Ping fiercely from the moment they left Guangzhou. She felt completely safe with him. The others in the *zhenying* felt much the same about Li Chen but strangers quickly became afraid of his temper and his intense stare. Throughout the voyage, he controlled his sister's every

movement, especially when she needed privacy. They spent days and weeks locked below decks in big seas. Buckets of salt water were lowered to them for washing and their toilet. At those times, Li Chen would position Li Ping between the ribs of the ship against the hull. When the sun shone through the cargo hatch, his sinewy body made a long shadow over her body. At night, the gimballed oil lamp cast his shadow wide. Li Chen stitched their hammocks together side by side. When they went on deck to prepare food or play Fan Tan or Mahjong with their travelling group, Li Ping would sit or squat just behind his shoulder. She rarely touched him – only when she needed him to hear what she wanted to say.

In the early days of the voyage, some passengers and crew taunted them, calling them Siamese Twins. Some asked Li Chen if his tiny brother had a tongue. But Li Chen's silent stare caused them to look away. Some just

laughed a little in a nervous way and moved on. But one evening, a member of another group from a village north of Guangzhou, a man much bigger than Li Chen, accused him of cheating at Fan Tan. Li Chen leapt at the man and pinned him to the floor of the hold. It took many passengers and crew to separate them. Li Chen was warned by the ship's captain that he would be put in the brig if it happened again. Later that night, Li Ping made Li Chen promise not to do that again. Though he never did, his reputation as a fierce man spread throughout the ship.

On windy days on board, Li Ping felt like a sea bird, sometimes sheltering from storms and sometimes flying above the waves. On sunny days, with the wind dancing and the ship running quickly before short, white-capped waves, Li Chen would play fast tunes on the *yueqin*, picking the strings with a bone that he had found on the deck.

Li Ping was sure her brother was making the ship go faster.

～

Later in life, Li Ping rarely spoke about the landing in Robe or the long walk to Ararat which took them many days – about twenty-five, she thought. All she would say was that the gold diggings were very hard work, and the special fees which only Chinese people had to pay to the colonial authorities made Li Chen furious. She also remembered European miners becoming so angry when her people found gold in places which they had abandoned.

In truth, the new arrivals from the Celestial Kingdom had little means of defence – other than prayer.

Most members of the *zhenying* maintained their traditional practice of praying on the full moon and the new moon after arriving in *Tsin Chin Shan*. There was much to wish and hope for. Li Chen joined the ritual more fervently in the Colony of Victoria than at home. In Guangzhou, he was following the wishes of his parents. In *Tsin Chin Shan*, his need for gold was so overwhelming that he prayed for luck as well as safety. Li Chen prayed quickly, never lingering at the altar. He bought three sticks of incense, lit them from a candle and then raised them quickly to his forehead. With a terse, hurried bow, he placed them in the sand-filled bowl beneath Guanyin and walked outside to wait for his sister.

Her slow observances annoyed him, and it was for that reason Li Ping stopped her practice of meditation and full prostrations on the full moon and new moon. She reserved her deeper expression of devotion for a daily practice, in private, in the tent she shared with her brother.

⌣

In their first winter and in the third quarter of the lunar cycle, between full and new moon, Li Ping knelt on the small mat which she had woven from long grasses. Guanyin sat on a small table between the beds of brother and sister. Li Ping had only just started to chant the Heart Sutra when Li Chen came through the folds of the tent doorway. She could smell alcohol.

'Why do you chant that nonsense about nothing being something and something being nothing? It makes me angry.'

'Dear Brother, I'm sorry if I annoy you. It's not my intention. I'm trying to help us all to live here successfully in peace.'

Li Chen softened at the sound of his sister's voice.

'Thank you, Little Sister, I know you have wonderful intentions, but the words of that chant annoy me and make me feel like a fool.'

Li Ping smiled and replied 'I'll try to explain – but only if you want me to and if you promise not to get angry.'

Li Chen rolled on to his bed with a shrug and a nod. 'All right', he huffed.

'Oh Brother, how to start?' Li Ping exhaled fully and then, with her next breath, she began.

'I see and feel two things in these words, although I still find them puzzling. The first is about how we use our thinking mind to try to find meaning. Perhaps it's like digging for gold. Finding a big piece is so hard, we fear that it's very unlikely, yet we know we could be standing on it at any moment in time. The more we work, the more tired we become but uncovering little nuggets keeps us hopeful. The little nuggets I've gathered from the Sutra by my mental digging seem to tell me that nothing stands alone. Everything depends on everything else. We can never escape into a world of our own. Even when we think we have.'

Li Ping saw Li Chen's eye lids flickering. His breathing slowed and deepened.

'The second thing I feel is more difficult to explain. It's the feeling that mental understanding is not all there is with anything, including the Heart Sutra. I feel something changes in my body as well as my mind when the words of the Sutra are formed and come out. Perhaps it comes from the concentration I've built up since my days in the temples in Guangzhou? Perhaps I've worn my resistance down over the years? Some days I can't even describe what I just told you a minute ago. But a feeling of stability continues anyway when I chant the words without trying to think about them.'

A snore from Li Chen filled the tent as Li Ping paused. His eyes were closed, his alcohol breath strong and unpleasant. But Li Ping continued resting her hand on the instep of her brother's bare foot.

'Dear Brother, I think it's best to think of these puzzling words as seeds. The Sutra is a planting and a watering. And the garden itself goes on forever in all directions. We can plant and water every day and the garden will never be overcrowded. And we'll always have the food we need. As the garden grows, the land is transformed, and it is nourished by the seasons and elements. What was bare and dry is awakened with new life. That's how I understand the final lines of the Sutra:

Gaté gaté pāragate pārasamgate bodhi svāhā.

Li Ping slept well that evening. She was pleased with her attempt to explain the Sutra, although she also knew that no explanation could ever be complete. And she was happy that Li Chen had listened and fallen to sleep when he did. Perhaps something of the Sutra would grow within him when he had no conscious resistance.

Proceeding Namelessly

By the time Li Ping and Li Chen got to Ballarat, their *zhenying* comprised thirty men and two women from See Yup. The size of the group meant that they could have their own space within the Chinese camp just outside the booming city. Their tents were set in groups of eight – four sets of pairs facing each other and sharing vegetable gardens, fireplaces and water barrels. Li Ping thought of her tent as a house within the inner walls of Guangzhou, and her countrymen's camp as within the outer wall of a new city just like the old one which she and her brother had fled.

Every morning and afternoon, she tended the garden. Each evening, she prepared meals from whatever food was brought to camp by the men working on the diggings or in the Chinese businesses setting up around the town. During the heat of the day, she walked slowly to the little piece of land within the camp set aside for a temple. Here, she held huge poles as straight as she could while men climbed them with ropes slung over their shoulders to lash roof bearers in place. She enjoyed the stillness of her task, standing at the root of this emerging place of worship for her people who had no other place to sense their past and practise their traditions. It made her feel strong.

One evening after dinner and just before sleep took hold of her, Li Ping wrote:

> *I see ten thousand objects. So many of them new to me, even in the night sky. It would take too long to name them all. Who wants to hear a muttering Celestial beneath the Southern Cross? Better I proceed namelessly.*

Li Chen returned from the diggings early every evening but rarely with gold. He talked about other ways of earning money and one evening announced exciting news about a Chinese businessman, Gee Loo, who had a grocery and laundry in the middle of Ballarat. He had obtained a licence from the British Colonial Government of Victoria to start an opera company with its own tent theatre. Li Chen told Li Ping that he had agreed to be a paid musician in the small orchestra for the touring opera company. When Li Ping said that she was worried about being left alone while Li Chen was away performing, he smiled and said, 'Sister, you'll be coming with me'.

The following weeks and months were joyful as they toured by horse and cart to the Chinese camps at Clunes, Avoca, Lillicur, Lamplough, Bet Bet and Talbot. At each of these newborn towns the company's tent theatre was set up, scenery rigged, costumes unpacked, instruments tuned and tickets sold in their dozens to their countrymen.

The Chinese loved it. The Europeans hated it. 'What's that infernal din?' they said to each other as they walked past.

Li Ping loved sitting in the back row watching the performances over and over. She never tired of the music and hearing Li Chen's beautiful *yueqin* playing. At times, she wished she were on stage too.

Li Chen found that being part of an orchestra did not just improve his skills on his instrument. It caused him to yearn for the simple, traditional songs of his childhood. His sister felt the same. In the cart on the way home, Li Chen would often play a tune on his *yueqin* while Li Ping sang softly next to him.

Li Chen found fulfilment as a paid musician for the first time in his life, and the extra money helped them to save the amount they needed to repay their father's debt. Li Ping tried not to add up their savings too often. It felt sad doing so and Li Chen always became angry at those times as he thought about the cost of the resident tax that only Chinese people had to pay.

At last, they made the eight hundred Tael to discharge the debt. Zi Yang, one of the soldiers of their *zhenying*, left Ballarat to take the money home to their parents in the Guangzhou. Recalling this later, Li Ping thought that it had happened about three years after they first arrived. She remembered counting three dry summers in a row without any rain and how, on the hottest days, she cooked small fish on sticks in the afternoon sun beside the western wall of their tent.

The day Zi Yang left was a hard day for both of them. They couldn't bear to share their feelings and thoughts about their parents and family. Instead, they talked about when, or if, they would ever attempt to go home. It was a regular conversation which never reached a conclusion.

However, on the day Zi Pang left, Li Ping realised something about her brother more clearly than before. She saw that Li Chen grew angry quickly because he felt trapped. He had lost face by being sent to *Tsin Chin Shan* where he could never be regarded as a real man. At home, he could be acknowledged but only if he returned with gold. But the little news they received from the

Celestial Kingdom gave them no encouragement – civil unrest continued; British colonial control had increased; more people were in poverty and a great drought had brought starvation to many counties. Li Ping was sure that he wanted to stay in the colony to prove himself.

The next day, after watering the radishes which were growing well for the first time, Li Ping walked to the temple site where a near-complete frame stood.

On her way, she recited from *Reading Zhuangzi* by Bai Juyi 白居易.*

> *Leaving homeland, parted from kin,*
> *banished to a strange place,*
> *I wonder my heart feels so little anguish*
> *and pain.*
> *Consulting Zhuangzi* 庄子, *I find where I*
> *belong:*
> *surely my home is there in*
> *Not-Even-Anything land.*

Her heart turned to Guanyin – the transforming deity – forming and reforming as both female and male, to bring compassion to the places of suffering.

⌣

In Ballarat, Li Chen met Paddy Mac, an Irishman and a veteran of the Eureka Stockade rebellion who played the

---
* Translated from the Chinese by Burton Watson.

mandolin. They became friends and in the evenings they played tunes in turn in the vegetable garden. Gradually, they learned to play as a duet. The slow, yearning melodies of the Irish tunes appealed to Li Chen's memory of the birds and waterways in the Celestial Kingdom.

But it was Paddy's racing jigs and reels and the bold upright rebel songs which got Li Chen's heart pumping. He responded with rapid-fire traditional songs of marching armies, especially a tune he composed himself about the farmers of Sanyuanli rebelling against the British when the Emperor's army surrendered. They told each other the stories of their songs in broken English as Paddy slowly picked up a little of the language of Guangzhou.

One evening Li Chen played 'Agony in Autumn', the quiet slow piece that he often played in the cart on the way home from an opera performance. He wished Li Ping were at his side to accompany him as he pitched his voice high and sang very softly and tentatively. Li Chen's absorption in the song overwhelmed Paddy with such feelings of hopelessness and unbearable longing that he came close to weeping.

Li Chen explained that the song was from *The Flower Princess* opera. It told the story of a princess and her husband who could not accept the new rulers who had overthrown the Ming Dynasty. Their despair was so great that they drank poison and died.

Paddy responded by playing songs from Ireland's

1798 Rebellion. Songs like 'Come All You Warriors' and 'Dunlavin Green' were played and performed with such strength and commitment that Li Chen could feel the air move around them. And, when Paddy sang 'The Minstrel Boy', Li Chen played along on his *yueqin* while Paddy plucked and strummed his mandolin.

Li Chen's head was buzzing when he crawled into bed after the session. It had finished with Paddy telling him the story of the Eureka Stockade and the cruel treatment of the Irish by the British in both the Colony of Victoria and Ireland.

In the morning, over a breakfast of potato and radish soup, Li Chen became agitated as he told Li Ping what Paddy had said. His speech got quicker and louder.

'We're the yellow Irish!' he said, stabbing his chopsticks into the mat. 'There'll *be* another rebellion here one day and we Chinese will be part of it.'

Li Chen picked up his *yueqin* and his fingers recalled 'The Minstrel Boy' and, within a few weeks, he mastered 'Kelly, the Boy from Killane'.

≈

It was a little after dark in the winter of 1859 when Li Chen burst into their tent where Li Ping had just lit their new iron stove made from plough shares and scraps of tin. Flames were beginning to lick and blacken the wok and soon the steaming root vegetables would be ready to eat. Li Ping worried that there was not enough food for them both. She thought about telling Li Chen that she had already eaten when he shouted,

'Look at this, Sister! A newspaper in our language and the language of the English. You're so much better with words than me. I think you can even read some English. Please, read it to me.'

Li Ping relaxed and then felt a wave of tension. She recalled how Li Chen never ate very much when he was excited in this way. And she knew that these moods would often be followed by an angry darkness.

The paper, when unfolded, was a large single sheet, much wider and longer than anything Li Ping had handled before. Li Chen was correct. The sheet contained English and Chinese characters carefully laid out and printed on both sides with a fold down the middle. The English words were clear and sharp. However, the Chinese characters were slightly indistinct, some even blurred. Li Ping thought that the Chinese sections resembled an ancient scroll, even an ancient dialect – such was the vocabulary and phrase construction.

Nevertheless, she could read it without much difficulty.

'Brother, where would you like me to start?'

Li Chen moved close to her shoulder and pointed. 'Can you read this? I think it's about what happened after the Eureka rebellion Paddy Mac was talking about.'

Li Ping took a moment to scan the article. It concerned many matters which Li Ping knew would enrage her volatile brother. Putting the paper on her knee, she said gently, 'Brother, perhaps you should eat first before I read it to you quietly'.

'No. I want to know now. There is something bad in this place, and I need to know. We all need to know.'

Li Ping removed the wok from the stove and began reading. The article opened with details about the new colonial regulations for Chinese miners which included limitations on Chinese residency and restrictions on immigration to the colony. It was some sort of Government announcement.

Li Chen exploded. 'There's nothing new in this for us. What are they talking about? No other people must bear these costs and restrictions. This paper is a disgrace.'

'Please, Brother, be patient while I read. I think the writer agrees with you. He makes his own commentary and says that the colonial government is being unfair.'

'The writer congratulates a man, Kit Chin, and nine of his friends for sending a petition to the government protesting unfair taxation of Chinese residents. This article says that the petition was sent on behalf of five thousand of our people here in Ballarat.'

'And he says that colonial courts should have interpreters so we can be understood properly.'

'Listen to this, Brother. This is what the writer says.

> *If some of our magistrates and one or two of our legislators had studied Chinese as a literary pleasure, even in a dialect not spoken here, and even although they should scarcely*

> *understand a word of what these Guangzhou Chinamen say, they would yet nevertheless be better able to understand Chinamen, and to make and execute laws that affect them.*

'Yes. This person really does support us. But it's not written by one of us. I can tell by the use of the characters. There's a European here in Ballarat who understands our condition in *Tsin Chin Shan*.'

Li Chen was not appeased. His suspicions about the motives and actions of Europeans were too strong to be placated by his sister's readings. He wondered if her comprehension was accurate. And whether she was honeying the language to calm him and mitigate the outrage he had felt from the beginning of their journey.

'Europeans tell stories to suit themselves – they even publish them. They use their stories about us to create laws which make living here impossible. Every chance I have had for success has been stolen by Europeans. I've lost face and cannot return to where I would be recognised as a man. I'm less than a dog in their eyes.'

Li Ping stifled a sigh of sadness and turned her attention to Guanyin to transform her discomfort with her brother's tensions and anxieties, particularly his way of blaming others for his life. Li Ping knew from their time in Ballarat that many countrymen had succeeded in businesses of many kinds, despite the obstacles and so much disapproval, even hatred. The vagaries of life, she thought, the roll of the dice, the missteps, the company you keep – the fortunes of life are so varied and unpredictable. She wished Li Chen could be more accepting of the world as it is and less blaming of others. Li Ping considered again the nature of conditions and the insights of karma. However, she could find no words of comfort for her brother – certainly none that he would accept.

Li Chen rose and stepped close to her shoulder again.

'What does this say?' he asked pointing to a small section on the back page.

'It is a statement searching for a person to carve printing blocks in Chinese and assist in translating Chinese and English for this newspaper. It offers payment for one day each week.'

Li Chen stood to attention.

'Sister, I know it is possible for you to do this. This is a great opportunity for both of us.'

Li Ping was shocked. How could her brother imagine such a thing? How could he leave her with strangers?

'Brother, I cannot say no to you. You know that. But can you see my fear?'

'Please, Sister, let me tell you about a Chinese miner I met two days ago. His name is Ah Moon and he was one of the hundreds of miners who went to Bakery Hill in protest at the colonial government's regulations and taxes. He helped to build the stockade, even though the European miners did not want him there. He pleaded with them to let him join the one hundred who barricaded themselves in their fort but he was rejected.'

'He was only permitted to watch as the British attacked. He saw a woman die and heard the wounded calling out for help. His heart was with them. His anger was the same as their anger. He was prepared to die. And he still is. But he has no comrades in arms now and never did. That's the truth we try to ignore.'

'Listen to me, Li Ping. We're poorer now than we've ever been. Our repayment to our parents has left us with nothing and gold is so hard to find. We've barely enough to eat, and still must pay more tax than Europeans on the goldfields. And they receive concessions from the government. For us, nothing! Worse than nothing. Soon, poverty will see us perish in this cold, hateful place.'

Li Ping put the wok back on the stove, opened the firebox door and placed more wood on the dying embers. More warmth stirred the evening chill. The silent siblings watched the fire and moved closer to the stove. Li Ping laid her hand on her brother's knee.

'I'm afraid to enter the European world so fully. I only feel safe alone or with you and our *zhenying*, dear Brother. Surely, I'll be exposed if I work in a printing shop with Europeans.'

Li Ping filled her brother's bowl with carrots and parsnips and ladled ginger broth over them. Li Chen ate quickly and hungrily, then putting the bowl aside said, 'I'll accompany you. The decision is made.'

Li Ping had never walked in the main street of Ballarat. She had only left the camp in the horse and cart with her brother when they made their way out of town to perform the operas in the mining camps nearby.

The roads from the camp to the city centre were muddy from overnight rains. Carts and carriages of all kinds sloshed through deep gutters and dung-filled potholes. Soaked horses nearly ran them down on their way to the printery. Li Ping's stomach churned from the smell of animal faeces and the blackened water running around their feet.

Europeans rushed past them at some distance. It was a relief to Li Ping that no one made eye contact. No one showed any interest in them at all.

Perhaps I'm invisible, she thought. And then, for the first time since arriving in *Tsin Chin Shan*, she realised how difficult this public anonymity must be for her brother, a man so driven to be proud. She remembered her father saying, when preparing her for her life as a man under Li Chen's protection, 'in *Tsin Chin Shan* they will never know – they don't want to be close to us anyway'.

Li Ping sheltered from a rain squall under the veranda while Li Chen went inside. Above the door hung a sign '*The Chinese Guardian*', in English and Chinese. Barely a minute later, Li Chen reappeared and ushered her inside.

A bearded European man, with kindly blue eyes, greeted her with a smile. As Li Chen announced 'This is my brother, Li Ping', the man reached out with his right hand. She had seen this European custom of greeting before. She bowed her head and froze. The man withdrew his hand and then bowed awkwardly.

'It is a pleasure to meet you. Your brother tells me that you read and write Chinese and English. You must be quite the linguist.'

Li Ping did not understand his last sentence. Panicking, she controlled the urge to run.

'My brother's very quiet and a very hard worker. Very quick to learn, Mister.'

'Well, that's a good thing indeed. Please allow me to introduce myself. My name is Jonathan Smith and I'm the proprietor of this printery and the publisher of the weekly newspaper, *The Chinese Guardian*.'

After a nervous in-breath, Li Ping spoke to a European

man directly for the first time.

'I am pleased to meet you, Ah Jonathan.'

She was surprised to hear her own voice and quickly scanned his face for his reaction to her tone and timbre, but the only response was a warm smile.

'Please, come this way, I'll show you around.'

They walked through a dimly lit room with an immense wooden desk overflowing with papers of all kinds: newspapers in English from around the district, files, letters and documents of an official nature.

The floor around a grand, diamond-buttoned leather chair was covered with books and pamphlets. An opened book lay on the seat of the chair. Li Ping recognised it as a poetry collection from the Tang Dynasty. The text was in Chinese.

Perhaps Mr Jonathan was reading this when Li Chen walked in, mused Li Ping, as they passed through the doorway into the printing factory. The air was full of the smell of ink and turpentine. Passing a paper stack nearly as high as Li Ping herself, she noticed another smell – almost a fragrance. It was the smell of the library in the Hualin Temple – the smell of paper in huge quantities.

'Paper is a miracle', Jonathan Smith announced, 'and your people invented it, I believe'.

He strode ahead, then turned and stood beside a remarkable steel and wood contraption with levers, stanchions and rollers all connected in some fashion never seen before by the siblings.

'This is my printing press which I built myself. I think it's the only printing machine in the world which can print in Chinese and English at the same time with wooden blocks of Chinese characters and metal type for English letters.'

'I had hoped to keep improving my Chinese by purchasing a set of Morrison's bilingual dictionaries, but I was told the Guangzhou printing factory was burned to the ground near the end of the Second Opium War just a few years ago. No new copies are available.'

'So, my alternative plan is to employ someone like you, Li Ping.'

Over the next hour, Jonathan Smith asked Li Ping questions about Chinese translations of English words. Her spoken English was hesitant and incomplete but her quick literary mind grasped meanings which she easily translated into Chinese characters. These, she drew meticulously in black ink on to sheets of white paper.

Jonathan Smith marvelled at the beauty of the script and the delicacy of the movements of her tiny hands and fingers. Smith could see that her hands had performed many years of manual work yet, despite such labours, retained their original fineness. 'So graceful and feminine', he thought.

Enchanted by this near-silent being who seemed to understand so much so quickly, Smith watched the siblings sitting together at the ink-splattered work bench in their identical loose blue tunics. Their long, shiny, black hair plaited right to left, hung nearly the full length of their backs.

'Can you carve the characters into blocks like this?' Jonathan Smith asked holding a blank, one-inch cube of wood and pointing to a row of tiny chisels and knives in a rack at the end of the bench.

'Li Ping will master this', Li Chen replied.

⁓

And so began a new life for brother and sister. Every Tuesday, they walked to the printery early in the morning. Li Ping assembled the galleys of Chinese characters and soon became adept at carving new ones as required. Li Chen busied himself around the factory, cleaning down the press and filling bins with waste products from the printing process. He stocked shelves with inks and solvents. But, whatever his task, he always kept Li Ping in view.

Jonathan Smith looked forward to Tuesdays. Even though his interactions with Li Chen and Li Ping were extremely formal, their presence lightened his mood. He had always been something of a loner, even at university in England, where his fellow students, both male and female, noticing his withdrawn nature, had encouraged him to join in social activities. But he was happier alone with his books, especially the translations of classical Chinese poetry. He loved the spacious phrasing and the raw, unembellished clarity of the texts. Their great evocations of the natural world sustained a solitariness within him. But, without their guidance and rhythms, he often felt deep loneliness.

⌣

The presence of Li Chen and Li Ping was like poetry to him. They lifted him, absorbed him. Li Ping especially. He knew that he was caught in a lust for the exotic, while publicly running a campaign for justice and equality for Chinese residents. Jonathan Smith was no stranger to the tensions between deep visceral feelings and moral values. He had worn this conflict continuously since puberty like an undergarment not to be revealed.

But he had also learnt to put these conflicts to the side. And would do the same again now with Li Ping, even though the beauty he saw in the svelte, diminutive being formed many a dream for him. Li Chen and Li Ping sustained his quest to create commercial and social connections between an ancient culture which he deeply admired and the fragmented, antipodean European world of the colony.

However, his efforts in the booming pioneering town were not always widely appreciated. Other businessmen around town called him 'googy' or just 'goog', as in a boiled egg – white on the outside and yellow on the inside. Sometimes, he almost enjoyed their insults. Your view of me is actually my aspiration, he told himself when hearing their mutterings around the town as he went about his business of bidding for advertising or distributing copies of a new edition.

～

In time, Li Ping looked forward to Tuesdays as well. She enjoyed the walk into town with her brother and trusted the kindness of Ah Jonathan, as she called him. He was generous in his payments and this regular income, though modest, made for new stability in Li Ping's life.

One Tuesday, Jonathan Smith called Li Ping and Li Chen into his office. Sitting in his diamond-button chair, he read from a report which he had received for publication.

'This concerns an Aboriginal man who was recently brought before the courts for stealing. It's his defence which I think will be of interest to you. This is what the magistrate said.'

> *This man has been in this district for three years, and the only instance of stealing I can otherwise remember was by a very intelligent aboriginal, who spoke English fluently; he was convicted and imprisoned for petty larceny twice within the year. I think that he learned this habit from the Europeans. I do not think it was his nature to steal.*

'The magistrate went on to say that, although he believes it is also not in the *"nature"* of the accused to steal, his defence of not being born in England and therefore not subject to British law has no legal basis and *'cannot be considered by this court – even though there is a semblance of proper moral argument implied by his assertion.'*

Li Chen jumped in. 'I believe the black man. He is correct. We were not born in England. We have no British blood in us. We should not be subject to laws by colonials who have no respect for anyone other than themselves.'

Since arriving, Li Ping and Li Chen had seen very few of the black people driven off their lands by the British, but this failed defence of the Aboriginal man resonated strongly with Li Chen.

It also deeply discomforted Li Ping as she pondered how the old cycles of suffering continued in this place. Even though the seasons were reversed in *Tsin Chin Shan*, nothing new had been found here.

～

Over the years, Li Ping became very proficient in translating Chinese to English and vice versa. So, when Jonathan Smith suddenly closed the newspaper to become a court interpreter, Li Ping went with him as his assistant. The formal nature of their relationship was easily maintained within the protocols of the court. Li

Ping felt safe, and Jonathan Smith continued to live in his dual world of unexplorable desire and justice for all. He felt safe too.

However, Li Chen's life began to unravel without those Tuesdays. His mining efforts were increasingly erratic and unproductive, nor could he manage his money and meet his tax commitments. His opium smoking increased and he resorted to money lenders to meet his debts while growing ever more secretive with his sister.

Li Ping worried about him, especially when he didn't return home, sometimes for days on end. But worry was no preparation for Li Ping when she arrived at court with Jonathan Smith to find Li Chen's name on the list of cases to be tried. He had been charged with manufacturing and selling fake gold and assaulting officers of the law.

A battered Li Chen was brought before the magistrate in chains. It was the first case of the day. Jonathan Smith instructed Li Ping that she could play no part as an interpreter and must sit in the public gallery if she wished to remain in court.

Li Ping sat as close as possible to her brother, who did not acknowledge her presence. He stared disconsolately at the floor and offered no defence. 'Guilty' was all he said in answer to the magistrate's question. And, before Li Ping could begin to reconcile what was happening, Li Chen was led away to serve five years' hard labour.

Outside the court, Jonathan Smith was moved to comfort her. 'What will you do?'

Li Ping remained silent for some time and then spoke strongly and clearly.

'I've been living without the support and protection of Li Chen for many months. The *zhenying* has been looking after me and will continue to do so till my brother is released and then we'll leave Ballarat forever.'

Little Wattles Love Raw Ground

Within days of Li Chen's release, the *zhenying* was on the road to Beechworth.

They walked from Ballarat for more than two weeks carrying everything they owned, either poled across their shoulders in sugar bags suspended from bamboo sticks, or in communal carts bought by the *zhenying* for the journey. These were the twenty-three Chinese who had arrived in the spring of 1873 – the year of the Rooster. Li Ping always remembered the last flowers of a japonica she saw in a garden on the south side of town when they arrived. She loved all flowering trees, but the japonica held special meaning for her. A large one stood about halfway between her parents' home at Kun Yam Hill and the nearby nunnery. When tired on a hot day, she would rest there for a while.

～

There were hot days as well on the long walk from Ballarat, especially when crossing the open plains east of Bendigo. One evening, she noted in her diary:

There is wind in the trees this morning. It's coming from the north. Gum trees rattle like parchment drums. Wattles whisper. My breath does too. One wind, many playing along.

When Li Ping and Li Chen reached the Main Street of Beechworth, they found commotion everywhere. Happy commotion: women and their children arranging pots of yellow and red flowers next to all the shops, men up ladders pulling banners across the roadway and Chinese people out with everyone else hanging banners saying 'Field of Cloth and Gold'. Carts and drays rumbled in from the east end of the town, loaded high with bundles of straw which were then thrown off to both sides of the street. Children, their mothers and grandmothers gathered and stacked the bundles to make a snaking golden fence on each side of the road.

Li Ping and Li Chen heard laughter in the spring sunshine. Li Ping's heart lifted as she sat in the cart waiting for Li Chen and the leaders to return from registering their arrival and obtaining permission to set up camp. The leaders brought news that the Chinese Protector would meet them shortly and escort them to the main Chinese camp known as Little Guangzhou. They had to move without delay because an event was about take over the streets.

The *zhenying* usually needed many days to establish a camp for twenty-three people, so Li Chen and the leaders decided to set up a basic travelling camp first while deciding on a permanent site. As the members of the *zhenying* scurried about – erecting the first tents, making the central fireplace and getting the kitchen ready – others from their homeland dropped in. But not to chat about recent gold strikes, or the lack of them. They only talked about the grand parade to take place in three days' time.

Hundreds of Chinese were already arriving from throughout the colony, even as far away as Sydney Town where news had arrived about the Chinese in Beechworth importing hundreds of pounds worth of processional paraphernalia from the Celestial Kingdom.

Just after noon on 12 November, the *zhenying* set off from the Little Guangzhou camp walking half a mile west up to Main Street and found a good place to watch outside the Post Office. Li Ping nestled in beside Li Chen. Street vendors moved through the crowd selling dumplings and skewered pork and chicken. Pannikins of expensive *Pua* tea were passed around by members of the See Yup society who came from Melbourne on the first train to Beechworth. Li Ping loved this day more than any other since leaving home. Even Li Chen seemed lighthearted sipping tea with his *yueqin* hanging over his shoulder.

'Brother, should you have joined the musicians in the parade?' Li Ping asked him.

'Not this day, Sister. We're newcomers. I don't need to play. I'm just happy for people to know I can play. Maybe later, maybe tomorrow. Who knows?'

The crowd kept building. Chinese and Europeans pushed together toward straw barriers. Fireworks and crashing cymbals signalled that the great procession was underway. Red and gold banners were raised, then came the shrine, smoking with hundreds of red sticks of incense. Lantern-bearers walked behind with soft deliberate steps, white silk canopies with embroidered birds and flowers were lifted to provide shade for the musicians playing the songs of the wild horsemen. Sedans encrusted with flowers carried elders and their wives, purple silk sedans carried more musicians, while young bare-chested acrobatic men tumbled and cartwheeled down the street.

Tomtoms thumped and, behind them, sixty or more men in traditional soldier tunics marched with curved broad blade ceremonial swords catching the afternoon sun. Behind, rode the emperor with his imperial guard dressed in blue silk tunics. As the fireworks spluttered on the ground, the procession finished with two men appearing dressed as warriors in full red steel battle armour covering them from head to knee.

The crowd roared in appreciation as Li Chen heard a voice of a kind he'd never heard before. He turned his head to the left to see two young horsemen standing head and shoulders above the Chinese crowd. Something about them reminded Li Chen of Paddy Mac. One cheered the soldiers on – in Chinese. The phrase he called out to the procession was quite clear to Li Chen: 'Seven blessings on you! Seven blessings on you!'

Li Chen couldn't take his eyes off the pair. The silent one seemed increasingly uncomfortable until finally he pulled his friend's arm, saying, 'Come on. Let's go.' As the Chinese-speaker turned to follow his friend, he caught Li Chen's eye, glanced at his *yueqin* and gave a smile. Not a big one – more for the instrument than for Li Chen.

~

After the parade, Li Ping and her *zhenying* went to the park opposite the courthouse and ate the noodles and dumplings which they had brought with them. Many groups of Chinese and Europeans found places to eat and talk about the marvellous things they had just seen.

Li Chen and Li Ping's *zhenying* offered food to a Chinese woman from Sydney Town who had travelled for days with her Aboriginal husband – a drover from the lands around the Gulf of Carpentaria. He regaled his Chinese audience with stories which astonished them. He talked of his grandparents trading sea cucumbers with the Macassans and their Chinese agents. He told them how very old Chinese coins, with holes in the middle, made good sinkers when he went fishing with his father.

And he finished with the most surprising story of all. One handed down through many generations of his family, about a Chinese admiral in an enormous boat who made many friendly visits to the drover's Saltwater people who looked after thousands of miles of coast and inland country.

'We believe that your people were the first foreigners to meet us on our country. Your people came as trading partners and you didn't try to take our country from us.'

The Aboriginal man concluded, saying, 'There are too many untold stories around this place'.

Once again, Li Chen found himself struggling with anger toward the overlords of the land in which he felt increasingly uncomfortable. He considered again the failed defence of the Aboriginal prisoner. Looking back toward the Chinese woman from Sydney and her tall black husband, he admired the man's obvious ease within the group and his lightness of voice.

'Could this friendship last beyond today?' he wondered.

A full party was now underway in the gardens. Some musicians from the procession arrived in their blue tunics and were welcomed by people offering food. An *erhu* 二胡 player and a young man with a sort of raw sounding clarinet called a *suona* 唢呐 joined Li Ping's small gathering.

Li Chen played along with his *yueqin*. They struck up 'Ambush from Ten Sides' – a fast song about the Battle of Giaxia – and then made the sounds of armies on horseback with their instruments. The European who had called out in Chinese walked past and started making a noise like a horse. 'Ye ha, ye ha, ye ha'. Then 'Go, banjo, go', he called, looking at Li Chen. In a mix of Chinese and English he told the musicians, 'There's a *cailidh* at the Hibernia Hotel at Sebastopol Flat in the Woolshed Valley on the last Saturday of the month. You should come along.'

He pulled a flask out of his pocket, took a swig, and kept walking. 'What's a *cailidh*?' they asked each other. No one knew, but Li Chen was determined to find out.

Back at the camp, Li Chen asked around about the man who spoke Chinese. He was standing outside one of the opium dens a day or two later when a smoker came out. Li Chen asked him if he knew the man. 'His name is Joe', the smoker said. 'He lives with his mother on a dairy farm in the Woolshed Valley next to the Reedy River Chinese camp. And he's a smoker.'

Li Chen and Li Ping felt good about Beechworth. The procession was the first public celebration of their culture that they had seen since leaving Guangzhou. The opera performances around Ballarat were enjoyable, though Europeans hardly ever entered the tent theatre full of Celestials. However, the grand parade was different. Their Chinese culture was on full display out on the streets, and everyone seemed happy to clap and cheer.

A couple of days after the procession, Li Chen made a trip into town to pay their resident tax and returned with a copy of the *Ovens and Murray Advertiser*. Li Ping read the editorial aloud to him.

> *The children of the flowery land were by far the best part of the show. They had spent some £800 on their costumes and emblems and so it could scarcely be wondered that they presented a most brilliant sight.*
>
> *They have grown upon us through their persistent energy, intelligence, and good conduct. The good feeling which now exists throughout this district between the Chinese and Europeans is due entirely to themselves, for we have been forced to recognise a civilisation different no doubt from ours but in*

many respects higher. To meet a Chinaman who cannot write his name is a surprise, and the difference of the Chinese children toward their parents, even in this district where the races are to some extent becoming mixed – women are always cosmopolitan – should be a lesson to some of our own colonial boys and girls.

There is a very marked change since the days of the Buckland riots, when ignorant Europeans looked upon them as something to be hunted down. Now a Chinaman is regarded as an equal in commerce and intellect, a superior in industry economy and sobriety.

When she finished, she tore the editorial out of the paper with great care and pressed it into eight folds so that it could stand upright on the small altar she had placed between their beds. The procession, the applause and now the editorial, gave Li Ping some relief from a knot which had formed when her father told her that she was to leave. It had grown tighter over the years when Li Chen was absent and became especially tight when he was in jail. But now in Beechworth, a freeing-up had begun. She even considered revealing her bodily gender. She was sure that some members of their group already suspected but, as time passed and everyone tried to turn survival into a ticket home, their curiosity faded. And there was nothing about the day-to-day life on the goldfields, or the colonial European settlements, calling for the woman in her to emerge. No men, children, family, habiliments or occupations. The more she thought about it, the more she realised that the freedom she most wanted was the freedom for her people to find a safe and harmonious home wherever they were, even in Not-Even-Anywhere-land. And, she thought, it should be the same for everyone in this place of wonder and fear.

The editorial's acknowledgment of the worth of Chinese people was also liberating for Li Chen, but in a very different way. He asked her to read again the sentences about Chinese intellectual superiority and business ability. On each reading, his confidence grew as he recognised that he might finally have the ability and opportunity to be successful, rich and admired.

Li Ping, however, feared that a knot of his was tightening as he clenched his fist, saying, 'Our days are coming, Sister!'

Oh, my Brother, Li Ping thought in her silence. You always search for more. Yesterday it was money. Today it's about us knowing your pain and your ambitions. It's time, dear Brother, to suffer in silence long enough to know that a tree or a cloud, or even my love for you, cannot be bettered.

~

Li Chen spent the next few days talking with other leaders of the *zhenying* about where to set up the permanent camp. They all agreed that they wanted to keep mining for gold. Li Chen asked about the *cailidh* too. He learned that it was an Irish music session held near the Chinese camp at Sebastopol Flat, where gold was still being found. Li Chen spoke to the leaders, and they agreed to inspect the area. When they returned, the *zhenying* packed up and, after walking ten miles, they found a location not far from Reedy Creek where, to their great surprise, nearly all the miners were Chinese.

But it was the beautiful market gardens on Sebastopol Flat which were most wonderful to Li Ping. She had never seen gardens like them in all the time she had been in *Tsin Chin Shan*. Rows and rows of cabbages and carrots and snake beans stretched back from Reedy Creek toward the rocky outcrops of hills forming the narrow valley.

The late afternoon sun shone straight down the valley, dancing across the granite boulders and the silver waters of the creek. The long, thin shadows of the pickers with the wide, pointy straw hats which they called *doulis* made her think of puppet shows from her childhood.

In the early morning, while the sun hung behind the eastern hills and the waterfalls, the pickers loaded carts to take their dewy vegetables to the hotels, eating-houses and stores down the valley. Li Ping's group negotiated with the other See Yup people who had established the gardens some years before, to work together. Some, like Li Ping, extended the gardens and the water races from the creek to feed new rows of greens and root vegetables. Most, though, joined the Chinese gold-seekers working over old diggings that impatient Europeans had left behind.

One evening back at the camp, Li Ping made a diary entry:

> *I love turnips. Watching them grow is better than eating them, even though they are delicious. The way they turn purple as they reach for the sun is beautiful and teaches me to keep myself covered here in Tsin Chin Shan.*

These were mostly happy days for Li Ping, who felt secure working in the gardens wearing her long blue tunic and her *douli*. The members of the *zhenying* turned their tents toward each other. They gathered split timbers from the forest and pieces of tin from the Europeans' deserted mining camps and used these materials to make their camp stronger and more comfortable.

But it was still often dangerous being away from the Chinese camp and the market gardens. Li Ping observed that many of the European miners suffered greatly from what the Buddha called the five great hindrances: desire, ill-will, poor concentration, restlessness and doubt. 'Together these lead to great jealousy and violence', she would say to Li Chen occasionally – but only occasionally, because he could become very impatient with her and stop listening.

One evening, not long after they had moved to Sebastopol Flat, Li Chen was carried back to the camp after a fight near the water race. He and some friends had been digging for gold in mullock heaps which European miners had deserted months earlier. A group of drunken Europeans called them 'scavengers' and 'opium addicts' and turned violent after Li Chen and his friends ignored their taunts.

But the worst violence and injuries occurred when the colonial police – 'the Traps' as they were known – arrived on horseback and trampled Li Chen and his friends. It was all over in a few seconds and the mounted police left while the drunks laughed and yelled, 'Go home, Celestials! Go back to your filthy joss house and opium dens.'

Li Ping almost convulsed when she was told of the violence. After she settled herself, she turned to her diary again and wrote:

This valley has suffered. It has been dug up and turned over for thirty years. What a shock it must be for this narrow soft place between the mountains when its stream and waterfall run yellow in the heat of summer. How hard it must be to feel fresh and alive with so many of its shady trees felled and its veins of clay once held within, exposed, and hardened in the sun. But the little wattles love the raw ground, and the boulder hills send new water when it rains.

Dear valley, after your gold, you will be alone.

Li Chen recovered quickly and went back to work, but his anger remained. Around the fire at night, he ranted about the injustices brought upon them by the same British imperial power which had driven him and his sister out of China. The British had gone to war to protect the market for their opium trade but, in the British colony of Victoria, their opium smoking was despised and only the Chinese were forced to pay a residents' tax. The hypocrisy so rankled Li Chen that Li Ping worried when her brother fell into these bitter moods of resentment and fury. It seemed that there was something inside him trying to eat its way out. Often, at these times, she would make tea and sit with him in a silent, simple way. Sometimes she would just sing and become a soft, cool cloth spread across his sadness and anger. She became as water to him.

Li Ping loved the temple in the camp, although it was not one of the Buddhist temples of home. Even so, it was a safe and familiar place to engage with the gods and the ancestors of all who had left the Celestial Kingdom, all who had struggled to find their way out of sickness or injury or debt. Each morning she took the short walk through the ducks and chickens to the little red sacred place. She would slip off her shoes and buy three sticks of incense from the old blind caretaker who sat just inside the doors in the low light that begins a day. He ran the coins through his fingertips and, with his head leaning backwards, he picked up a handful of sticks in his left hand. He selected three sticks, one by one with the thumb and first finger of his right hand. His long fingernails looked like snails.

Li Ping also loved the Guanyin in the little temple of tin and wood. The Bodhisattva of Compassion looked down from the altar as neither he nor she but as both he and she. They, Guanyin in woman–man union, and Li Ping, the sister as brother, had their moments together before the day started. She would bring the three burning sticks to her forehead, kneel and place them in the bowl of sand at the feet of Guanyin. Her three prostrations were slow and complete. She didn't simply kneel and bow forward as most did. She stretched herself out fully, her feet reaching toward the door, her head, arms and hands reaching toward Guanyin. Some days she felt as if she could stay there forever. Some days, when she could feel Li Chen's anger in her, she felt like rushing away. On those days she would prostrate herself fully, whispering toward her stomach, '*gaté gaté pāragate pārasamgate bodhi svāhā*'. As she rose from the floor, her arms wide, her hands coming together as she reached her full height, she appeared in the low light of the temple as a rice paper fan, opening and closing and then opening again.

One morning when Li Ping stepped out of the temple, she noticed the old caretaker sitting on a bench to the right of the entrance.

'I've heard your brother is planning to go to the music session at the Hibernia Hotel on Sunday night', the old man said.

Li Ping nodded.

'Tell him that the Irishman who invited him has good and bad in him. Yes, good and bad. And more than most.'

'Be careful. Remember the Heart Sutra. Form is emptiness and emptiness is form. I see you know that the same is true for everything.'

Li Ping was startled by the reference to the Heart Sutra. Her mind was on the old man's earlier comment about Ah Joe having more good and bad in him than most.

She chanted the sutra silently as she walked slowly back to the camp, 'no suffering, no origination of suffering, no extinction of suffering, no path, no understanding, no attainment'.

'How can this be?' she asked herself again and, as always, she returned to the chant, this time creating a rhythm between the words and her steps.

'Yes. Nothing exists on its own. Not even suffering. Not even not suffering. Nor good or bad. What is the nature of a man who has an abundance of both?'

Longing That Cannot Be Separated

After a night of many short sleeps, Li Ping sipped tea and put aside the thought of breakfast. Still foggy, she began to write.

> *It was so hot last night I could not sleep. I became impatient with myself. So many stories began to tell themselves, whether I wanted to hear them or not. Who is this storyteller?*

Li Chen had not told Li Ping his plans, but that evening, with his *yueqin* over his shoulder, he took his sister's hand and headed for the Hibernia. Even before seeing its lamplights, they could hear the music filtering through the young wattles sprouting against the hotel's slab and mud walls.

Li Ping felt nervous doing such a dangerous thing. She had never been inside a hotel but had seen men drunk. Their faces changed. Their laughter changed. Their voices changed. Their movements were slow and fast at the same time. The air around them stiffened. They made Li Ping want to crouch down and stay close to Li Chen. Walking through the door, they saw a circle of players and singers, maybe eight or nine. A big tin oil lamp burned in the middle of the room and their drinks, next to their boots, looked like huge, polished jewels. Another fifteen or twenty drinkers sat and stood around them. She saw more people in the dark corners ahead.

A fast tune finished. Some light applause. A few men moved towards the bar when the young Irishman, who had extended the invitation, saw them. He jumped up and called out, 'Banjo! Sit here.' He shuffled the circle of chairs around until Li Ping sat next to Li Chen, who was next to the Irishman. Li Chen unpacked his *yueqin* and put its case under the chair.

'Drinks?' asked the young Irishman.

'Thank you, but no drink', said Li Chen.

The Irishman leaned across Li Chen and looked

straight at Li Ping, who shook her head slowly and lowered her gaze to the damp, dirt floor. But in that brief glimpse of the Irishman, Li Ping saw something. Not just the ocean blue of his eyes or the fact that she had never seen blue eyes so close to her before, barely two feet away. It was the way they seemed to shine from inside. Consciously deepening her breath, she felt the cool of the in-breath in her nostrils, just as she would in meditation. Breathing in, she saw the eyes again seemingly alight.

Breathing out, she cooled again as the image faded.

'Who's your mate?' the Irishman asked.

'My brother, Li Ping. He is very shy', Li Chen replied.

'Nice to meet you, Lee. You too, Banjo. Can I call you that? I'm Joe. Joe Byrne.'

Then the music began, an Irish rebel song that Li Chen had heard Paddy play and sing before. It was a strong song, not fast, not slow. Like a thrusting fist. Li Chen played along quietly. A few musicians smiled as they took an interest in the unfamiliar twang of his *yueqin*, or 'banjo' as Joe called it.

Joe sat back in the circle. He had no instrument, just a few pieces of paper rolled up in his right hand with which he beat time on his thigh, urging the players on. He was like the conductor of an orchestra.

Li Chen became increasingly confident with each verse and chorus. The other players began looking for him and, when the last chorus came, Li Chen played with force and accuracy. Even his body movements became bigger as the song ended. Li Ping had never seen her brother like this before. She had experienced his burning intensity when alone with him, but not so demonstrative or loud, and never with a room full of Irishmen. He seemed at home here and she wondered whether he would desert her one day.

The music continued, and the drinking. They heard many songs about Irish rebellion against the English. The crowd loved them and so did Li Chen. The room became noisier and noisier but, when Joe stood up, the room fell silent. He put his hands in his hip pockets and, unaccompanied, sang a song which was to become a favourite for Li Ping.

I wish I was in Carrickfergus
Only for nights in Ballygrand
I would swim over the deepest ocean
Only for nights in Ballygrand
But the sea is wide and I cannot swim over
And neither have I the wings to fly
I wish I had a handsome boatsman
To ferry me over, my love and I.

My childhood days bring back sad reflections
Of happy times there spent so long ago
My boyhood friends and my own relations
Have all passed on now with the melting snow
So I'll spend my days in this endless roving
Soft is the grass and shore, my bed is free
Oh to be home now in Carrickfergus
On the long road down to the salty sea.

Now in Kilkenny it is reported
On marble stone there as black as ink
With gold and silver I would support her
But I'll sing no more now till I get a drink
Cause I'm drunk today and I'm seldom sober
A handsome rover from town to town
Ah but I'm sick now my days are numbered
Come all me young men and lay me down
Come all me young men and lay me down.

After Joe finished singing, the musicians packed up and the drinkers began to leave. While Li Chen was putting the *yueqin* away, Joe asked him quietly if he had a smoke. Li Chen nodded and, speaking in Chinese, which Joe easily understood, said he had opium at the camp where Joe would be most welcome.

Talking a mixture of English and Chinese as they left the Hibernian, Joe spoke mostly about how the police were always following him and the Irish families, especially the Catholics. Li Chen told Joe about his friend, Paddy Mac, and the British bombardment of Guangzhou years ago.

'We yellow Irish – you white Irish', Li Chen said.

Joe laughed and slapped Li Chen's shoulder, 'Good one, Banjo. Well said, China!' And he laughed again louder than before. Joe tried to explain that there was an expression in English, 'China plate', which meant 'mate'. Li Ping could not work it out at the time but, when explained to her many years later, she laughed a lot.

∽

Back at the camp, members of the *zhenying* gathered around. It was rare for a European to enter their space in the Woolshed Valley at Sebastopol Flat and they were very surprised to hear Joe speak Chinese. The opium smokers shared their pipes with the young man so full of energy and having such clever ways of saying things. Everyone stayed up late and talked about being sick of their treatment as likely criminals and sick of paying unfair, racial taxes which they could barely afford.

Joe told them that he was named after his grandfather, an Irish rebel, a guerrilla fighter from County Carlow, who had been transported for life to Australia. The group was fascinated to hear colonial history told by the young Irishman. They paid close attention to his description of the Irish rebellions in Australia, at Castle Hill and Ballarat, which the colonial authorities had put down.

'The next one won't be put down', said Joe drawing heavily on the pipe. Ah Hoy, who had mined in California in the 1850s, grew very excited. He clapped his hands and ran around the group, yelling, 'The British are coming; the British are coming!'

The whole *zhenying* jumped up and looked around in alarm till Ah Hoy started laughing and sat down. Over the next hour or so he told them what he knew about the American War of Independence and how the Americans drove the British out of the country and became independent. And thirty years later were again at war with the British, who burned down the American President's house. But the Americans fought back and the British eventually retreated. Ah Hoy told the group that the American wars started because of unfair taxes and the cruelty of the British Government.

As Li Ping went to bed, she noticed Li Chen and Joe behind the fire leaning toward each other talking aggressively, though not at each other. She noticed Li Chen's anger intensifying and worried that the British powers in *Tsin Chin Shan* would be determined not to lose again. Of course, she thought, the more people they punish, the more will oppose them. Li Ping felt that the cycle of violence could escalate quickly at any time and many lives, including their own, would be endangered.

She found the prospect of rising conflict very difficult to bear. Fear rose in her body. Her chest tightened and her stomach churned. On this evening, the symptoms were mild: a tightening around her rib-cage and her heart beating fast. Li Ping concentrated on her breathing as she lay down to sleep, searching her memory for the sutras which explained karma. Without texts at hand for so many years, she struggled to recall them verbatim. However, she considered the nature of an intention to be as important as any knowledge or action. What, she wondered, would be reborn from rebellion, should it occur?

As she fell asleep, the words of Sister Abbess came to her: 'Whatever I do, for good or for evil, to that I will fall heir'. Next morning as first light shone between the bark walls and across her forehead, she found herself reciting an old text that she could only partially remember.

> *According to the seed that is sown,*
> *So is the fruit you reap therefrom,*
> *Doer of good will gather good,*

Doer of evil, evil reaps,
Down is the seed and thou shalt taste
The fruit thereof.

Li Ping's community changed after the night Joe entered the camp. More and more conversations took place about the harsh laws cruelly enforced by the colonial authorities. Joe's *qi* was running through her community. She could feel it in all of them, especially Li Chen who spent hours with Joe, playing music and smoking pipes. Joe even taught him to ride a horse fast through trees and boulders on the steep hills each side of the camp. They galloped along the edge of the water race that went directly into Joe's mother's property at a terrifying speed.

Sometimes she watched Joe's mother herding her cows with a big stick, yelling to get them into the shed for milking. Mrs Byrne was kind to Celestials and offered to exchange milk with them for cabbages. Li Ping hated the taste of milk but was happy to give Mrs Byrne as many cabbages as she needed. Mrs Byrne showed her the beautiful vase she had been given by her cousin's husband when Joe was born. 'Nothing for the girls, you know – and there's six of them – but old Demon Donnally took a fancy to Joe and gave him this which he reckons is Chinese and very old.'

Li Ping ran her fingers around the top of the vase and observed the fine blue illustrations painted on the white porcelain. 'It is very beautiful, Mrs Byrne. I hope Ah Joe admires it.'

'Well, at least he didn't break it in one of those tempers he had as a child. He's been a trial for his mother, Li Ping, a never-ending trial and there's enough of them in our lives up here without him making trouble like still mixing with that Kelly family. They're always in trouble with the police and even the mother's been in jail. And more than once.'

⁓

Ever since the great procession of 1873, the community of Beechworth became interested in displays of Chinese culture, especially Chinese New Year celebrations when the huge dragons would come out and dance. One year, perhaps 1876, Li Ping and members of the camp, including Li Chen, went into Sebastopol Flat to meet other locals about arrangements for the New Year celebrations a few months away. On their way home, they were set upon by a group of men leaving the hotel. Li Ping could never fully recall what happened. She remembered being abused and called ugly. Her next memory was of Mrs Byrne leaning over her, dressing the wounds on her neck and shoulders and her badly bruised left shin.

'Don't try to move – you're safe with me', said Mrs Byrne.

Li Ping's tunic had been removed and she lay nearly naked on a thin flock mattress. A lamp burned beside her, casting light on her chest and on the slab wall of a bedroom. The rest of the room was black. She smelled eucalyptus on her skin and, from a little farther away, the milky waft of a European. She heaved and convulsed as Mrs Byrne rolled her on to her side to vomit into a chamber pot. The sudden movement tore at Li Ping's pelvis and legs, and pain shot through the length of her spine. Her legs felt like strands of molten fencing wire.

'The doctor will be here in the morning', Mrs Byrne told her.

Li Ping was in shock. Her seven thousand days of presenting as a man were over. She felt no panic about this, nor did she notice Li Chen's absence. Something about Mrs Byrne's kindness and control affected Li Ping: the way her hands touched her wounds, her face in the lamplight, her voice asking Li Ping not to move. Li Ping felt the bodhisattva in Mrs Byrne. This almost silent woman from Guangzhou had never been touched before by a European woman – not even accidentally – but Mrs Byrne's care gave her a feeling of love which she had not felt since childhood.

From her bed during the following days, Li Ping watched Mrs Byrne as she came in and out of the room with soups and stews and breads and ointments. She noticed that Mrs Byrne's body was thicker and wider than her mother's and her voice was loud and raw when she yelled at people or animals from the back door.

But it softened when she stood alone stirring pots and singing the same song which Joe had sung at the Hibernia, but slower and with some different words in the last verses.

But I'll spend my days in endless roaming
Soft is the grass, my bed is free
Ah, to be back now in Carrickfergus
On that long road down to the sea
I'll spend my days in endless roaming
Soft is the grass, my bed is free
But I am sick now, and my days are numbered
Come all you young men and lay me down.

Though she loved Mrs Byrne singing softly in the distance, it made her sad thinking about her own parents and her old home. She was now thirty-five years old and had been in *Tsin Chin Shan* for nearly twenty years before meeting Mrs Byrne. The feelings of loving care which she had experienced, combined with the void of separation from her parents and homeland, agitated and choked inside her. Li Ping felt that she was falling away from Guanyin and knew she needed her temple. When trying to recite the Heart Sutra, her mind spun away to childhood days. *Gaté gaté* sounded like a trick.

⌣

After being bed-bound for about a week, Li Ping was told by Mrs Byrne to get up and start walking around. Movement, she said, was necessary for her recovery but Li Ping remained silent.

'You can't stay there forever', Mrs Byrne said. 'You must get up after breakfast or I'll get you up.'

Li Ping knew that Mrs Byrne would do what she said. Later that morning, as Mrs Byrne held her firmly around the waist, she took short steps out of the little bedroom and into a bright cold early spring day. Frost lay in the shadows under the eaves of the bark-roofed hut. They sat on split logs as Mrs Byrne peeled oranges from her little orchard.

That sunny day, Li Ping told Mrs Byrne everything – from her earliest memory of the scroll on the wall of the bedroom which she shared with her brother, to hiding behind her brother to pee in a bucket on the rolling ship. And everything after that. She couldn't stop, even when it seemed that Mrs Byrne did not understand. When Li Ping couldn't remember the right word in English, she would say it in Chinese, even full sentences while looking straight into Mrs Byrne's eyes. Her voice grew loud with excitement as she talked about the days travelling through Ballarat with Li Chen and the opera company. But she was too ashamed to speak of Li Chen's prison term.

'Why haven't you gone home after all these years?' asked Mrs Byrne.

Li Ping explained that having repaid their parents, Li Chen could only face going home if he became rich. 'After nearly twenty years we're still poor, and the gold is running out. We were lucky to be able to send the money home when we did.'

Mrs Byrne asked Li Ping how she felt about what had happened over all the years.

'Very hard question, Missus. I have felt so many things. Now I worry about my brother so much. I need him very much, but he also needs me. I wish he could see that. No matter how much I try to help him, he always wants something more, or something less. Nothing is enough for him. Not even me.'

Mrs Byrne's heart was moved by Li Ping's story. She wondered how long this tiny, injured woman-man could carry such a burden.

Li Ping continued, 'Life isn't just desires and feelings. I've been taught that it's about being conscious of the eternal force that we come from and return to. I've had to live by not being caught by strong emotions and thoughts but being open to the compassion of Guanyin – even being the compassion of Guanyin when I can.'

Li Ping took a long time to say all this. Margaret Byrne had never heard a story like it before. Towards the end, Li Ping wept when telling Mrs Byrne that she and Li Chen had never received a letter from their parents since leaving Guangzhou. The only word they had ever received was years ago, when a family friend arrived in Ballarat from Guangzhou to tell them that their parents were relieved to be able to repay the money lender. They also said that they hoped Li Ping and Li Chen would have enough gold to return home before too long. The final words of the message were that their father promised to write soon. But there had been no contact since and they had not nearly enough gold to return as successful 'sojourners', as the Celestials were often called in the colony.

Li Ping and Mrs Byrne met regularly following their talk. Li Ping walked beside the Chinese water race crossing the Byrne property to deliver fresh vegetables to Mrs Byrne, who offered butter in return. Li Ping didn't like butter at all, but Li Chen liked to use it to fry the fish he caught sometimes.

Mrs Byrne told Li Ping that her husband had died from a heart attack six years earlier, when she was a month pregnant and caring for six children. And he left her with a run-down dairy farm to manage. One of her brothers-in-law died recently, and the other, the clan leader, John, had left the Woolshed Valley and moved to New South Wales. The eldest male in the family was now Joe, who was little help since he rarely came to the family farm.

Mrs Byrne resented her son's careless, free and easy ways. Occasionally, Li Ping would see him riding fast through the gully and up the water race through thick bush with his friend, Aaron. They nearly knocked her over one day when she was carrying Mrs Byrne's flowers to Sebastopol to sell at Ah Han's grocery. The horses reared and Joe jumped down to see if she was all right. He apologised in Cantonese for scaring her. Reaching his hand out, he said that his mother had told him all about her. Li Ping had not seen his face in daylight so close to hers. She noticed that he was agitated and torn in some way, yet she felt perfectly safe in his gaze, though his nervous and unsure manner left her uncertain as to whether he wanted to talk more or just go. Their brief encounter ended after Joe asked Li Ping to tell Li Chen to meet him outside the Hibernia about six o'clock.

Back in the garden, on a stool between the rows of ripening corn, Li Ping wrote:

> *Young men on horses shake the ground. Between the trees a cloud of dust shows the way they went at full speed going nowhere, touching nothing except the animal and its will to run. What's at the end of this? A long draw of water? Cool air for wide nostrils or just a longing that can't be separated from anything else?*

Joe did not turn up that night but, a few days later, when Li Ping was delivering vegetables to Mrs Byrne, she was told Joe had been jailed for stealing and killing a cow. Mrs Byrne was overflowing with anger. Anger at Joe, the police, the courts, her dead husband and the opium dens that Joe visited. Li Ping listened to her fury and understood how saddened this strong woman was about the way her life had unfolded. Mrs Byrne felt that she was losing her eldest child. The one who had been so clever and close to her when young but had become reckless, even dangerous, in recent years.

'Oh, I'm sorry, Missus', said Li Ping gently. 'But you can still see the young boy in him. We feel his warmth. I do too.'

Mrs Byrne remained grim, her shoulders dropped a little as she bent her head forward and said, 'Warmth will not feed his sisters but he'll be fed in jail'.

Li Chen was also angry when he heard about Joe's jailing, but his anger was directed towards the colonial authorities. Only a few days before Joe was jailed, Ah Hoo was imprisoned for fighting with a gang of local white boys who had tried to rob him. One boy, who had fallen heavily during the fight, was the son of a wealthy squatter who told the court that Ah Hoo had kicked his son in the head when he was on the ground. However, Ah Hoo testified that the boys had circled around him and pushed him from one to another, trying to make him giddy so that they could take his purse. He called them 'wild dogs'.

The squatter objected loudly, saying that Ah Hoo was an opium addict and a pickpocket who had approached the boys to steal their money to buy his disgusting drug. 'They're cunning vermin, your Honour', he told the judge who later jailed Ah Hoo.

Li Chen was so enraged by the imprisonment of Ah Hoo and Joe that he called all the members of the *zhenying* together. Over a dinner of noodles and fish, Li Chen spoke angrily about the treatment of the Chinese and the Irish by the colonial courts.

'They hate us so much, they've now passed laws stopping any more Chinese coming to *Tsin Chin Shan*', he told them. 'They hate us being here.'

'They hate us at home too. Look how they've sent their people all over our country to make their opium trade. They go anywhere, even to small villages far from the ports they've stolen from us. And, when we fight back, they use that as an excuse to take more ports.'

'Look what happened', he continued, 'when the villagers in Tengyue tried to stop the Britisher, Margary, from making a trade road right across our country to bring more opium from Burma. We were forced to sign the Yantai Treaty 烟台条约 – another treaty to give up more ports while also stopping us from taxing the foreign traders.'

Li Chen then read out a section of a Chinese newspaper quoting a recent speech in the British Parliament:

> *A few months ago, we seemed to be on the eve of another war with China, which, if it had broken out, would have been the fourth war we have waged against the Chinese within one generation. Now, the question arises – Whose fault is it that our relations with that country are in so disturbed and unsatisfactory a condition? Well, a thorough-going and unscrupulous patriotism would say*

without hesitation, and with great emphasis – It is entirely the fault of the Chinese; they are an arrogant, insolent, treacherous race of barbarians, or semi-barbarians, who know not how to keep faith or observe Treaty engagements, and they have come into contact with us, an upright, honourable, law-abiding people, who are always faithful to our obligations, and who have shown the most wonderful forbearance towards them; while they are resisting, by cunning and chicanery, our efforts to introduce among them the germs of a higher and better civilisation than their own.

Li Chen's anger was so fierce that the group split in two and Ah Fang spoke.

'These are not things we can change', he said. 'There's no point in making ourselves angry or sad. We must concentrate on our work and our businesses so we can look after each other and our families. We must stay true to the *Daodejing* 道德经 and what the great teachers, including our parents, have taught us. We must work hard and show respect to everyone, not worry about what they might think of us.'

Li Chen replied, 'We know no one will ever help us. Why think the world might change just because we know how much we are its victims? We must act with force and purpose. If you want to be a good quiet Chinaman, that's your choice. I want to change things.'

'Brother Li Chen, we understand your feelings', he continued, 'but you're walking the wrong path. This is not the *Daodejing*', Ah Fang continued. 'The sage Confucius says, "If you do not have the Dao yourself, what business have you spending your time trying to bring corrupt politicians into the right path?"'

Li Chen replied, 'Confucius is dead in China. We are alive in a place where we and others – like our Irish brothers and sisters – can be strong together. In China, there's only the Chinese to fight the British monsters. We have been hopeless on our own in our own country for many years. And we still are.'

'But here in *Tsin Chin Shan*, we can have allies', he told the listeners. 'Look how the new settlers in America defeated the British. They got rid of them. And look what happened at Eureka and at the big meeting of miners at Chewton – the miners made the authorities change things. They were beginnings – not ends.'

Listening, Li Ping felt love for her brother as her belief in the truth of the words by Ah Fang and the sage tightened like a knot in the bottom of her belly. Without talking to each other, both Li Chen and Li Ping recalled their father's bitter criticism of the Qing Dynasty, its failure to protect its people and the heroism of the farmers of Sanyuanli when they rose up, unsupported, during the First Opium War.

Over the years, Li Chen had maintained close relations with Chinese trading companies sending gold back to China and importing Asian goods for Chinese communities in *Tsin Chin Shan*. Through his contacts, he knew about the conditions back home: the poverty, famines, growing unrest and the hatred that people felt for the British and the other foreign powers who had made themselves rich while humiliating a nation. Li Chen raged on at the *zhenying* and asked if they knew that the British now even used a Chinese word to describe someone who is too weak to fight.

'They laugh at us and demand we *kowtow*. They use our own language to show their power over us', he seethed.

Li Chen then said something which silenced the entire group. 'China now has a child Emperor. How can a boy fight the British? There's no future for ordinary people with a child Emperor, and there's no future for us fighting colonial powers alone. The colonials are too strong, and our Emperors are too weak. There's no one to protect us other than ourselves. We must stand up and resist like the farmers of Sanyuanli and the miners of Eureka. But we need allies and, when Joe comes out of jail, we'll join forces', he announced.

After a long silence, Ah Fang spoke. 'This is not The Way', he said. 'This is not the Dao.'

'We will see. We will consult the *I Ching* when Joe returns', said Li Chen.

Mayday

Last spring, when birds were warbling,
I thought of my brothers, young and old,
Now in autumn, as chrysanthemums decline,
I think of my own birth.
Deep green rivers make me weep,
The dust of battles covers the land.
What a pity! Within a hundred years
The capital city of Xian was destroyed.

(From Han Shan's Cold Mountain Poems)

Joe was released after six months but did not return home. He worked with his best friend, Aaron Sherritt, making improvements to Aaron's selection. Occasionally, he would take a break sitting on a rock shelf looking down into the Woolshed Valley. From there he could see his mother's farm and, just beyond that, the vegetable gardens of the Chinese camp. Sometimes, he saw his mother and sisters moving their dairy cows around and doing the chores that he once did. Distracted by feelings of guilt, he disposed of them by knocking out his pipe and returning to help Aaron. Together they felled trees and split their trunks for fence posts and slabs to lay across the soggy sections of the track leading up to the hut. Aaron wanted his selection to look smart enough to welcome the upstanding citizens of Beechworth in their jinkers.

One day, a month or so after being released from prison, Joe watched the little stooping bodies and faded straw cone hats of the workers in the Chinese gardens. They were picking something. He wondered what had ripened and which gardener was Li Ping.

After finishing with Aaron that day, he said no to a brandy and lemonade, jumped into the saddle and turned his much-loved mount, Music, toward the bush track winding its way down to the Chinese camp. No ordinary rider or horse could handle the steep rocky cliffs and boulders but, within twenty minutes, Joe reached the post and rail gate into the Chinese gardens. He leaned forward, his forearm across the pommel of the saddle. Tilting the brim of his hat down to cut out the low afternoon sun, he saw four identically dressed Chinese workers walking toward the gate. He felt certain that the second one was Li Ping and wondered how he could be so sure. Something about the way a female body moves, he thought, no matter what sort of clothing they wear.

As the workers reached the gate, Joe slid off Music. The first worker passed by without acknowledgment of any kind, but Joe tipped his hat anyway, saying, '*nihao*' with his customary confidence. Joe could see that the worker behind the first man was Li Ping. He removed

his hat fully and, with a bow that seemed a fraction too deep, said confidently in Cantonese, 'Good evening, have you had a good day in the fields?'

Li Ping was startled to find herself face-to-face with Joe at the gardens. His accent intrigued her, as did his choice of words which made her laugh a little.

'Why do you laugh?' he asked in English.

'Because you just asked me if I have been taking a bath', she replied.

'Well then', said Joe. 'That means I've already conveyed to you the reason for my visit. Would you do me the honour of teaching me to speak better Cantonese?'

It was not the sort of decision that Li Ping could answer without consulting her brother, so she suggested that Joe come with her to meet Li Chen. He was overjoyed to see Joe. They shook each other by the shoulders.

Li Ping explained what Joe had requested and Li Chen became serious, his eyes sharpening.

'Yes', he replied. 'You can learn from my sister. But I want your help in return.'

Li Ping knew what Li Chen wanted from Joe and it worried her. She knew that they both could be killers if certain conditions arose.

Just two days later, while Li Ping was washing her hands and face in an old tin bathtub in the back corner of the garden, she saw Joe arrive on Music at the gate down past the rows of spinach and the tall corn plants soon ready for picking. She patted herself dry, brushed off her tunic, put on her *douli* and tied its red sash under her chin. Walking to the gate, she thought about the first lesson and wondered what Ah Joe wanted to learn. She recalled him mixing intonations in a way that completely changed the meaning of words but was amazed that it did not happen more often. His ability to get the upward and downward tones of the language was unusually good for a European. Perhaps it had something to do with his love of music and singing? She smiled to herself when she remembered the name of his horse. He must have a very good ear, she thought, as she reached the gate.

The heat of the day had passed. They sat in the vegetable garden and Joe spoke first and quickly: just a simple 'hello' in Chinese. She detected his nervousness and sensed that he was trying not to make the same sort of mistake as last time. Li Ping brought the palms of her hands together and bowed toward him. Lifting her head, she replied with the same simple greeting. She noticed that he was wearing town clothes, not working clothes, and that his boots were shiny. He wore a red kerchief around his neck and his sparse and sandy beard moved a little in the late afternoon breeze. His eyes held her directly and easily. His in-breath was quick and deep. He had become nervous.

For the first half-hour they walked slowly together through the rows of vegetables, identifying them by their Cantonese names and talking about growing cycles and the health of the plants. Li Ping introduced Joe to other workers they met along the narrow paths between the beautifully tended beds.

They walked past a small lotus pond next to an open tin tool shed. Joe had never seen such order and beauty. Tools hung in descending order according to their length, hessian bags tied with red, yellow or green sashes. Jars of seeds lined the walls. And, in the falling afternoon light, the pink and white lotus flowers were beginning to close.

As they reached the little orchard in the back corner of the garden, Li Ping invited Joe into the octagonal gazebo. The roof was thatched with dried reeds from the creek. The sides between the load-bearing poles were open. Two hammocks were slung from the poles and two low stools stood in the middle next to a table holding a white and blue jug and two cups of the same design.

Li Ping motioned for Joe to sit, saying 'Please', in Cantonese.

She poured two cups of lotus root tea and, smiling at Joe, took her seat next to him. As they took their first sips, she noticed how he had waited for her to pick up her cup. His nervousness had fallen away. Now quite calm and not anxious to speak, he was at ease absorbing the light and the sounds of the garden.

'May I now comment on your Cantonese?' she asked him.

'Yes please', he replied confidently in Cantonese.

'Your accent is good', Li Ping began. 'And you understand the tones and the pitch quite well. I have not heard many Europeans speak as well as you. And your vocabulary is good too. I can see you have used Cantonese a lot to buy things. How do you want to get better?'

Joe shifted nervously on the stool, leaning forward and back, sloping sideways a little.

'I want to speak it more. I want to do more than just name things and talk about basic things like the weather and things to buy.'

'I'm happy to help if I can. What would you like to talk about?'

There was a long silence. Joe's gaze shifted over Li Ping's shoulder as he looked past her, up the hill toward his mother's farm and the family home.

'How is your mother, Ah Joe?'

He dropped his head a little.

'I don't know. I haven't been home since I got out of jail.'

'Why is that, Ah Joe?'

'Because she wouldn't help me in court. The magistrate asked her if I had been good to her, and she said she couldn't say.'

Li Ping responded, 'I think your mother has to work very hard all the time'.

'Yes', he nodded.

Shafts of dipping sunlight cut through the gazebo's open sides – its poles casting long shadows into the paddock beyond the garden.

'Look', said Joe. 'There's a Chinese farmer with eight legs over there.' He pointed to the elongated shadow of the gazebo on the ground. Then he laughed and jumped up, strong and cheery.

'Can I come back next week for another lesson?' he asked.

'Yes', Li Ping replied.

She brought her palms together and bowed to him. Joe did the same, though his bow was rushed and shallow – a type of nod really. And then he was away, off on his horse, Music.

Li Ping was surprised to feel so comfortable with him. She was more fearful of Europeans since being attacked, even though she couldn't remember the details, only the deep roaring voices and the way they hissed and spat, 'Celestials!' The memory of that sound reminded her of great gum trees splitting and falling in a storm. But she could see that, if it hadn't been for those angry men, she would not have met Mrs Byrne ... and her son.

Li Chen was in many minds about consulting the *I Ching*. Perhaps he had laid a trap for himself? If the ancient oracle gave a negative response about rebellion, how could he find and accept another way? But if the oracle was positive, he would have to proceed even though, at this stage, he did not have the forces or a plan. In any case, did he really believe that an ancient book from

China could have anything useful to say about *Tsin Chin Shan* today?

As a youth in Guangzhou, he took no great interest in the *I Ching*, but there were changes in his life which seemed very much like the predictions and readings made by the old Taoist priest that Li Chen's father consulted every week. In the presence of Li Chen's parents and in his family home, the ancient *Book of Changes* was part of life, no matter what the private thoughts of any individual person were. It was held by everyone in some way. But here in this land where no Asian or European knew anything at all about what had happened before their arrival, the Great Book seemed like a lost thing.

But he had said that he would do it and the others would hold him to it. And if a reading of the *I Ching* were to be taken seriously by his countrymen, he would require a very knowledgeable interpreter of the ancient text. Li Ping expected Li Chen to ask for help in finding a qualified reader of the oracle. She was not looking forward to the discussion but was dutybound to always support her brother, just as she felt a duty to Guanyin in every conscious moment. She wondered how she could best help Li Chen.

'Can the old man at the temple do the reading and explain it?' Li Chen asked after breakfast one day.

'Dear Brother', she said, 'first you must be very clear about the question you wish to ask. It is a mistake to seek "yes" or "no" answers for yourself. The oracle talks about what's happening which *can* change. Think hard about your question, Brother. It's pointless to ask "Can we defeat the colonial power?" or such questions. Even an unasked question in the back of your mind, such as "Will a favourable answer get me more support?", can take your attention away from the bigger truths.'

She added, 'The question must allow for understanding of conditions that exist and coexist – whether you think them helpful or not. Please, Brother, come to the temple with me and we shall sit with this together.'

Li Chen refused and withdrew from Li Ping and everyone else. He spent his days sluicing for gold with a small group of friends. They made little money. He played no music and spoke very little. He was like a fire smoldering in evening drizzle as a deep, disconnected brooding enveloped him. Li Ping wondered if he had commenced the final descent which had been threatening since he was a youth. She had seen other Chinese people lose their connections to life in *Tsin Chin Shan*. Separation from the homeland, a desperation for wealth and the back-breaking work of endless duration to obtain it, was, she knew, a destructive mix. And unbearable for someone like him, a Celestial, as if from another planet or even universe. A resented alien. Each time that Li Chen entered this realm of withdrawal, his descent was quicker and deeper than the time before, and this time – for the first time – his face changed in an alarming way. It became blank.

⌣

Joe did not return for his lesson the following week. Li Ping realised that the discussion about his mother had made him search for something else to talk about. She heard that he was back in court after fighting with Ah On, who had ordered him and Aaron to stop swimming in his dam. In the fight following, Joe and Aaron were beaten with bamboo sticks and retaliated, breaking the bones of Ah On's face with a rock.

Mrs Byrne saw it happen and this time spoke up for Joe in court. Later, when Li Ping was having tea with Mrs Byrne, she read out the editorial from the *Advertiser* concerning the trial. It said, '*We remind these two strapping lads of the fate of the bushrangers, Smith and Brady, who commenced life like them and ended on the gallows*'.

Li Ping could see that Mrs Byrne thought the same could happen to her son.

The bond between the two women grew as Li Ping spent part of each day helping around the dairy farm. She often tended a small vegetable patch that she had made for Mrs Byrne to provide a constant supply of greens for her children. They were mostly little cabbages and 'weed spinach', as young Margaret Byrne called the 'green stuff' that her mother had started mixing into soups and stews.

Li Ping grew to love Mrs Byrne's cows. Though she had never developed a liking for milk, or anything made from it, she loved the slowness of the animals and smiled to herself when watching them chewing and rolling their eyes at her. To her, they appeared to smile and eat at the same time. Her mind would often then flick to Li Chen's fast slurping of his noodles, and she wished that he could enjoy them like a cow chewing her cud. Blossom was her favourite cow and Li Ping loved watching her huge swaying black and white belly and great fleshy udders as she made her way into the milking shed untroubled by anything.

Li Ping was weeding the radish patch the day the police arrived again looking for Joe. They announced that he was wanted for murdering a policeman. She heard Mrs Byrne say, 'He's made his own bed, now he can lie in it'. When Li Ping looked up, Mrs Byrne was staring at the policeman with her arms folded across her chest. She said nothing more in answer to their questions. Her jaw was shut so hard that Li Ping could see bulges beside her ears. Mrs Byrne did not move at all until the last of the police galloped out the gate. Then her shoulders started to shake. Li Ping walked toward her, but Mrs Byrne turned quickly and went inside.

⌣

A few weeks later, Li Chen returned to the camp in a frantic and angry mood. He had seen posters all over the Woolshed declaring the Kelly gang outlaws. A reward of five hundred pounds was offered for each of the four gang members: Ned Kelly, Joe Byrne, Dan Kelly and

Steve Hart. Li Chen's rage at the actions of the colonial authorities, and his deepening sense of fellowship with the Irish, had brought him back in touch with other sympathisers.

Barely a month later, the gang robbed the bank at Euroa and distributed cash to people who needed help, including Mrs Byrne. The authorities rounded up followers of the gang and, without charges being laid, jailed them for up to three months. Anyone the police thought had supported the Kelly gang had their applications for land denied.

Troopers and police moved through the Woolshed Valley putting up more 'Wanted' posters and demanding that people turn in the Kelly gang. The police cautioned that any suspected sympathisers would be jailed without trial. Some were also threatened with loss of their mining licence, or the permits needed to run businesses. Others were told that they would be deported if they did not tell everything they knew. And the Byrne farm was watched more closely than any other place in the valley.

Li Ping could feel the tensions rising everywhere she went. At the Byrne farm, the children and their mother showed a renewed defiance as Mrs Byrne took a reluctant pride in her hunted son. Beyond the Chinese camp, in the shrinking community of Sebastopol, where gold was getting harder and harder to find, and the mood was similar. Everyone seemed to know someone who had been jailed for sympathising more with the Kelly gang than the murdered policemen and the traumatised witnesses to the robbery in Euroa. Rebel songs were sung loudly at the Hibernia as a sense of change and unease ran through the valley.

Li Ping turned her mind to the *I Ching – The Book of Changes*, as the Europeans and others called it – and contemplated her own question. She needed guidance. In the small anteroom on the western side of the temple, Li Ping placed the three old Chinese coins in the palm of her right hand. Speaking her question aloud – 'What can't I see in my situation?' – she closed her hands together, shook the coins and allowed them to fall. The old caretaker at the doorway felt each one, declared either head or tail and recorded the value: 3 for heads, 2 for tails. Li Ping repeated this six times to create two trigrams according to the rules of the ancient book. The final calculation from the text passed down over three millennia was:

> 27 I/The Corners of the Mouth (Providing Nourishment)

Placing his hand over the *I Ching*, the old man eased his fingernails between the pages of the text, and gave his commentary:

> The inquirer provides nourishment for men of worth and thus reaches the whole people. When things are held fast, there is provision

for nourishment. The 'corners of the mouth' means providing nourishment for what is right.

Turning to the summit for nourishment and deviating from the path to seek nourishment from the hill brings misfortune.

The source of nourishment is awareness of danger. It brings good fortune. It furthers one to cross the great water.

Li Ping knew what must be done. They must stay on the path of awareness for liberation to become possible.

⌣

Within three weeks of Li Ping's readings, the Chinese community of Sebastopol Flat were excited to hear that the Kelly gang members had returned to their secret hideout in the rocky country southeast of the Woolshed Valley. After robbing the bank in Jerilderie, they burned the mortgage documents of struggling people indebted to the bank and again distributed money to the poorest families in the district.

Li Chen rushed to share the news with Li Ping and talked quickly and loudly about getting their group together to help the Kelly gang remain free. His energy had returned, and Li Ping felt both worried and relieved.

Together they made many preparations over the

following days and weeks, beginning with a meeting in the middle of the camp to identify and delegate tasks. Ah Fuey and Meng Zi agreed to arrange food and other essential supplies from the local grocer, butcher and baker. Ah Qei took responsibility for blankets and clothes. Others agreed to stockpile tobacco, brandy, rum and ammunition.

Li Ping and Li Chen accepted the task of informing the Kelly gang, through their families, that they were supported by the local Chinese community. But it needed to be done carefully. The Byrne property was being watched by the police from the rocky outcrops to the southeast of the house paddock.

However, Li Chen was confident that he could find a way in. He was sure that the police could not see the water race from their vantage point. He also knew that Joe was able to move unseen through the nearby hills by using the old Chinese gold-carrying tracks which Li Chen had shown him years before. He had joked with Joe at the time that the Chinese were the best bushmen in the diggings because they had to remain unseen to avoid being set upon and robbed.

But Li Ping insisted that it was too risky for her brother to enter the property and talk to the family. Instead, Li Ping whispered the message of support directly to Mrs Byrne while she unloaded her regular wheelbarrow load of vegetables. 'Our people want to help Ah Joe and his friends. Can we meet?'

Two days later, Li Chen found a handwritten note in the butter delivery from the Byrne dairy. The note requested Li Ping and Li Chen come to the milking shed at ten o'clock the following Wednesday evening, a dark night with no moon.

The people of the Celestial Kingdom knew that it was never completely dark in the bush. Since arriving in *Tsin Chin Shan*, they had been moving from place to place after sunset without the lamps carried by Europeans. The threat of assault and robbery was ever present. Lamps could be seen for miles, so far better to let the eyes and other senses adjust. Their ears and cheeks became very sensitive to changes in the air close to boulders and large trees. On cloudy nights with no moon, many people of the Celestial Kingdom could walk a well-known track by memory of past steps.

On the night Li Ping and Li Chen set off for the milking shed, the sky was clear, the stars of the southern sky were sharp, and the earth was quickly growing cold. A wind threatened a change from the west, probably bringing rain with it. Li Peng noticed her breath on every step as Li Chen kept moving ahead of her and then stopping and waiting impatiently.

The milking shed was open to the west and was catching the wind. As Li Ping approached, she could see two men in the corner of the shed: one sitting on a stool, the other standing. It was Joe standing and he motioned for Li Ping and her brother to come closer into the corner so as to introduce the other man.

'This is Ned Kelly.'

Joe and Ned had put up blankets on the slab walls to stop any chinks of light being seen by police from the rocky hill half a mile away. Joe lit the stub of a small candle stuck in the bottom of a tin pannikin. The four of them sat on milking stools in a tight circle around the little flame which struggled in the wind. Joe spoke quickly, saying that he wanted Li Ping and Li Chen to tell Ned about the bombardment of Guangzhou and how they came to be in the colony.

Li Chen said that it was a waste of time. 'There's too much to be done to keep you free.'

But Joe grew agitated. 'Li Chen, listen. There's something you need to understand. Ned's been talking to supporters who hate Celestials because they take their jobs.'

'No', replied Li Chen abruptly. 'Chinese people don't take jobs from anyone; we make jobs for ourselves. Who's spreading this poison?'

'Wait, Brother', urged Li Ping. 'Please listen. Ah Joe wants to talk.'

In the momentary silence after Li Ping's intervention,

all four warily pushed themselves back a little on their stools and caught each other's eyes. Joe continued.

'Ned's very protective of everyone close to him. So, he wrote to the Premier of New South Wales demanding that his colonial government send all Celestials home and stop more coming in. I made a copy. I knew we must talk about this.'

Joe pulled a sheet of paper from his hip pocket and read the final section.

> *Now, Sir Henry, I must tell you that highway robbery is only in its infancy. The white population are having their jobs stolen from them by this inundation of Mongolians. When the white man is so driven by desperation, death and destruction will follow. It's up to you to control our borders and send these Celestials back to their country as a lesson to the hordes threatening to invade us, threatening to take our work and our land. I present my respects to the Sydney police.*
>
> *Yours E. Kelly*

Li Ping hung her head and breathed out slowly, repelled by threats of violence even though she understood the desperation of the hunted men whose behaviour was like their father's when the British bombed their home in Guangzhou.

Joe continued. 'Ned needs to know what the British did to you, and you need to know what he wants to do with them. It's very dangerous and very risky but his plan won't work without support from all the victims of England's colonial rule here. And that includes you and your people.'

Li Chen looked at Li Ping, who began by talking about their mother and father and their house in Guangzhou. Ned stopped pacing as Li Ping described the British navy coming up the Zhujiang River to bomb their city into maintaining the drug trade. Ned sat down on his stool between Joe and Li Chen as the brother and sister took turns to tell their story. Li Ping spoke in a low, soft voice that drew Ned forward, and Li Chen hissed with anger about their people's moments of humiliation: the poll tax, the residents' tax, their treatment on the ship. He also told Ned about his friendship with Paddy in Ballarat and the songs that they had played and learned together.

'We are the yellow Irish', said Li Chen. The story stopped there.

Joe looked at Ned as Li Chen stood up, walked behind his stool and leant against the wall. Li Ping sat upright, her back as straight as a strainer post in the corner of a paddock.

Ned took over. 'Perhaps you're the best allies we could have. The bastards chasing us won't even consider we'd accept protection from what they call "the yeller fellers".'

Li Chen and Li Ping looked at each other as he continued. 'They'd never believe that there's a chink in our armour', he said with a gauche laugh.

Joe was embarrassed but it didn't stop him laughing with his leader.

Li Ping and Li Chen looked at each other bemused.

Then, reading the faces, Ned said respectfully, 'We would very much like your people to join us'.

And, after a pause, Ned stood up and half-turning his back, he added, 'Please'.

Joe sucked in a breath, smiled at Li Ping, then nodded lightly toward Li Chen. Ned returned to his stool and explained quickly that they were planning a military-style action against the colonial government to form the Republic of Northeast Victoria.

'It should have been done at Eureka for the whole colony', he said. 'As I said in the Jerilderie letter, it will pay the government to give the suffering people justice and liberty. If they won't, my actions will certainly open the eyes of the Victoria Police and the whole British army.'

'Joe helped me to write some words I have committed to memory.'

> *I give fair warning to all who have reason to fear me, sell out now and give £10 out of every hundred towards the widow and orphan fund. Leave Victoria in as short a time*

as possible after reading this notice. Neglect this and you will suffer consequences. I am an outlawed widow's son and my orders must be obeyed.

'My letter from Jerilderie had no effect other than allowing us to be legally killed on sight and enabling the persecution of anyone supporting me.'

'I thank you for being with us. We will raise the flag of victory over these tyrants with your help and support, which is accepted with gratitude.

'Meanwhile, Joe will see you again soon with a date to meet near Greta to finalise our plans.'

⌣

Joe did go to the camp as Ned suggested, but not to talk about the date of a meeting in Greta. He went to see Li Ping.

Li Ping did not recognise him immediately. What she saw appeared to be a tall Chinese man wearing a *douli* and riding a beautiful grey, squeezing carefully between boulders and down steep shale drops recently dumped by rockslides. No one rides a horse in country like that, she thought. And then she knew it was Joe. He always got off his horse the same way, patting its neck before taking his feet out of the stirrups and sliding to the ground. He never left the animal until he rubbed its face to reassure it of his return. Li Ping's heart was warmed by the care he showed to Music.

Joe left his horse in the bush, just back from the garden, and walked through the trees to the east until he was opposite the gazebo. He struggled to get through the post and rail fence with the *douli* on his head and took it off as soon as he was safely under the gazebo. Li Ping knew the great risk that he had taken in coming to the camp by passing within a few yards of search parties and their Queensland Aboriginal trackers patrolling silently through the hills almost every day. He could have been killed on sight, by anyone.

Li Ping put her hoe down on the newly tilled garden bed and walked slowly toward the gazebo, stopping at the water tank to wash her hands and face. She bowed to Joe as she came under the shelter, and he bowed to her. It was a proper bow – not too shallow, not too deep, neither fast nor slow. She wondered if he had been practising somewhere.

They smiled and he spoke first.

'How do you like my clothes?'

'Yes, Ah Joe. Where did you get them?'

'Your brother and a couple of his friends brought a suitcase to our hideout a few days ago. Most were too small but this just fits, I think. Must be some big Chinaman somewhere, eh?'

Li Ping smiled at his free and easy humour as she considered his breadth and the tight fit of the tunic.

'Can we speak Cantonese together now?' asked Joe.

'Yes', she replied. 'But we must stay here under the gazebo, at least until the sun goes down further.'

'How should we start?' Li Ping asked.

'I'm not sure. Can you ask me a question and I'll try to answer it without making you laugh?'

Li Ping smiled and dropped her head a little.

'Ah Joe, can you tell me, in Cantonese, how to ride a horse?'

Joe looked very surprised. 'That's hard. Much easier to show you. I'd love to do that.'

'Maybe one day you will', Li Ping said. 'But now I'd like to hear you describe how a human and such a huge animal work together.'

Joe felt something poetic in her request. Could he remember a song or a poem in praise of that union, one he knew so well, a union which fitted him better than nearly all the other relationships in his life, so far?

'Try please', Li Ping said. 'Just short sentences, if you like.'

'Have you ever heard a horse's heartbeat?' asked Joe.

'No', Li Ping replied. 'I don't think I've ever been close enough. I'm a little afraid of them.'

In Cantonese that Li Ping could understand, Joe said, 'To ride a horse, you need to hear the horse's heart. It knows. Pat it nicely on its left side. Put your face close to its chest beside its front leg. And your ear on its body, there. If you have a good ear, you will hear, *bah lub*, *bah lub*. Do this before you try to get on.'

'Very good, Ah Joe. I understand you', she said with a warm smile. 'Very good Cantonese.'

Li Ping noticed Joe's smile in return and that the colour of his cheeks had reddened.

She was unsure as to whether she should comment on the young man's reaction, but before coming to a fully conscious conclusion she found herself saying, in Cantonese, 'Ah Joe, I think you are blushing'.

Joe did not understand till Li Ping raised her fingers to her cheek and said in English, 'Blushing, Ah Joe, blushing'.

Joe took a long, slow breath and held Li Ping in his gaze. Words stalled in the way they used to in his early adolescence.

Li Ping smiled. She led him to a stool where the informal lesson and conversation unfolded by Li Ping asking Joe about the things he loved. First, he talked about his male friends and the hotels they visited. Sensing that this was not the right topic, he shifted to Irish songs and places in the bush. And then he talked about his youngest sister and why his horse was called Music.

'No horse has rhythm like Music', he explained as he continued to speak about his love of writing – especially poems – and how rhythm was important to him. Joe saw Li Ping was impressed by his love of poetry and she told him that she too was a lover of verse.

'Can you recite a Chinese poem to me?' Joe asked.

Li Ping pondered and then recited a poem in Cantonese. Joe listened carefully. She could see his eyes following her mouth. His blue eyes almost danced as her language produced a music he had noticed before. She wondered if it was his ear for melody causing his eyes to light up. When she finished, he clapped and then bowed.

'Can you translate it into English or would that spoil everything?'

'I will try. It's called "In Spring" by Li Bai. It is very old.'

Your grasses up north are as blue as jade,
Our mulberries here curve green-threaded branches;
And at last you think of returning home,
Now when my heart is almost broken …
O breeze of the spring, since I dare not know you,
Why part the silk curtains by my bed?

'Beautiful, so beautiful', said Joe, clasping his hands together between his knees and rocking forward on the stool. 'Thank you.'

Li Ping continued quietly and slowly with a mix of English and Chinese.

'All natural things, like the spring and the wind and us, come from the eternal force that changes everything many times over. It shows us that we renew the way for ourselves as we listen deeply. Desire and longing are here with us as well. So are fears. All of this can come to rest. All of this can change. All this can become love and care – like you have for your horse. Like you listen for its heart. Like you want others to listen to your heart. I think you understand, Ah Joe?'

Joe listened quietly as her voice mingled with the whisperings of the breeze now stirring the bush. As the sun reached that moment before twilight when the tall, straight white gums glowed orange, something similar occurred in Joe and in Li Ping.

She stood first and waited for Joe to rise. Li Ping brought her hands together and bowed and he responded in kind.

Joe was at ease in the momentary silence which followed their bowing.

And then Li Ping spoke. 'I must go, now. Thank you for coming.'

~

Within a week of the discussion with Ned Kelly in the dairy shed, Ah Wong, the head man of the camp, called the community together outside his sprawling humpy.

'There'll be a meeting here tonight at eight o'clock with Police Detective Fook Shing', he announced. 'He has some important things to say about the Kelly gang.'

Li Chen and Meng Zi tried to ask questions of Ah Wong, but could see it was pointless even before their words were formed. The head man was adamant that nothing more would be said until the meeting with Fook Shing.

Some members found it hard to believe that a Chinese could work for the police, let alone be a detective, but a few already knew him from his days as a theatre producer in Bendigo.

'Not the same man', said the duck farmer, Ah Loon.

Candle and lantern-maker, Ling Zi disagreed. 'I was in the Bendigo camp with him when he was head man', he said. 'He liked dealing with Europeans. We could never work out if he thought they were smart or stupid. But I'm sure he thought that he was smarter than them.'

Li Chen and his closest allies worried about a possible informer in the camp and discussed who in their community might be prepared to forsake countrymen to collect the reward for the Kelly gang. If the traitor had already given up their names, the meeting would be nothing more than a trap to arrest them. Or perhaps to round up a large number to detain in Beechworth prison along with the other sympathisers already jailed without trial.

Li Chen walked the paths of the camp all afternoon looking for any sign on any face which might reveal treachery. He sat on a flat rock and watched a group of old Chinese sluicers wading in and out of the Reedy Creek a few yards away. As he identified each one by name, he assessed the likelihood of their culpability. No names stood out.

Li Chen arrived early at the Ah Wong's hut. Sitting on a cut log, he watched the community arrive down the narrow paths fanning out in four directions from the centre of the camp. Some carried small mats, while others, like Li Ping, brought a tea pot and a cup or two. Each found their sitting or squatting place – some in pairs, others in chattering groups. Li Ping knelt next to her brother who accepted tea just as Ah Wong lit two lanterns outside the red and yellow front door of his tin and bark abode.

Fook Shing. *Illustrated Australian News*, 13 November 1880.

In the falling light of day and the rising light of lanterns an unusual-looking Chinese man emerged and faced the crowd. Li Ping had never seen a Chinese man present himself like this, wearing a spotless black fedora, tipped from left to right, his pinstriped suit coat was pushed back by his left hand deep in his pocket, exposing a ruby silk embroidered waistcoat the same colour as his loose full lips. He wore a French shirt with a winged collar and a bow tie. All in all, he had the stance of a European at the races and the whole effect produced a scattering of applause from the gathering.

Fook Shing smiled, acknowledging the applause, and told them, 'You know, in Melbourne they call me a civilised specimen. Ha!'

'If only they knew I was just like you but without the bedpans', he paused, and semi-squatted, 'to uh, sluice for gold'. He rose smiling at his stagecraft and laughing with a few of the miners who wondered if the comedy was an insult.

Li Chen looked around to see who laughed and who looked like they were used to his jokes but, quick as a flash, the joker changed the mood.

'I'm here to give you a warning', he said.

'I've identified your leaders in this valley and others throughout the northeast of the colony. Within a week they'll receive a letter from me demanding they tell me who's been helping the Kelly gang. Either that or face arrest and jail without trial. Based on the replies, I'll make a report to Commissioner Standish.'

The detective withdrew his hand from his pocket and did up his jacket preparing to finish.

'I expect every reply will say the same thing: that you know nothing. Make it that way. That's all I have to say at the moment. Let's have a pipe now.'

Most of the gathering were suspicious and began leaving for their huts, but not so Li Ping who was certain that a man living successfully in two worlds must depend on both worlds to survive. She could imagine the detective using his knowledge of their community to bring a pickpocket or burglar to court, but the arrest of so many countrymen would forever destroy his credibility with his informants and his people. With them gone, he would be of no further use to his employer, the police. Plainly, she thought, Fook Shing had well-rewarded skills in the balancing act which had so handsomely paid his tailor.

Li Chen was suspicious of Fook Shing's *bonhomie* and remained seated on the log waiting to see who would take up the detective's invitation to share a pipe. Meng made the first move and Li Chen stepped up to join him. A few more moved forward between the lanterns and finally Ah Wong opened the door of his hut and they all moved inside.

As pipes were filled, Fook Shing took off his new hat and looked around for a place to put it down safety.

'There is an informer', he said still holding his fedora. 'He's a grocer in Mansfield who was asked by a couple of members of the See Yup society to donate provisions for the gang. He's one of those Chinese who thinks he can be successful all on his own if the police like him.'

This information made Li Chen and the others nervous. Sure enough, Mansfield was a long way from the Woolshed and the Kelly gang's hideouts, but whispering by merchants had caused big trouble for gold-digging clan members previously.

'But don't worry', Fook Shing told them. 'Standish is a colonial fool. I met him first in Bendigo when he was the Chinese Protector. No idea about how things worked in the camp. And no smarter now that he's in charge of the police.'

'He was planning to get local black trackers to find the gang till he was told of Ned's childhood friendships with the Natrakboolok people. That's why he decided to get Native Mounted Police from Queensland to join the search. Believe me, they won't find anything. The Aboriginal people in this area who haven't been moved into missions will do whatever they can to put the Queenslanders off the scent.'

'But I can tell you two things are certain', he continued. 'The Traps will never find the Kelly gang, and my bet is that the Kelly gang will find them. Do you agree?'

Li Chen, afraid of what others might say in answer to such a dangerous question, decided to speak first.

'As you said at the meeting, we don't know anything. You were right, Mr Detective. Light the pipe and relax. Tell us about the opium houses in Melbourne. Ours is very basic, as you can see, but I hear that some in Melbourne Chinatown are very superior.'

'Well, my favourite is behind the King Wah restaurant in Little Bourke Street. It's beautiful and doesn't deserve to be described as a "den" by all those righteous European newspaper editors. I'd call it a palace. The embroideries and scrolls take you back home with every draw on the

pipe. The lounges are soft silk and broad enough for female company and entertainments. There are different musicians every night to ease the beautiful slide into ecstasy. It's a much more refined and sensuous place than the Prince of Wales Hotel with its rum and raspberry drinkers, or even the stuffy Melbourne Club from where that fool Standish tries to run the police force.'

The conversation switched again and again over the next two hours and never returned to the Kelly gang. But the detective from Chinatown in Melbourne did say that the Melbourne newspapers were outraged by his gambling habits and his opium smoking.

'But my superiors support me and told the papers I needed to smoke and gamble to do my job. I mean, how else could I find enemies of the government without a little bit of fun mixing with you taxpayers?' He laughed and called for another pipe.

Li Chen recalled Li Ping's comments about Fook Shing living in two worlds. She was correct. And Fook Shing had a way of keeping both worlds on edge.

Within two days of Fook Shing's return to Melbourne, Mrs Byrne visited the Chinese garden with cream and butter in exchange for new corn cobs bursting from their silky husks. Li Ping gave Mrs Byrne enough to make a meal for her whole family. As Li Ping filled the basket, neatly placing the cobs side by side like little swaddled things, Mrs Byrne leaned close and whispered the date, time and address for the meeting at the township of Greta.

Li Ping would not go to Greta. She was worried about the impending violence and suffering that the men would endure, especially Li Chen. It was painful to see her brother's energy become so strong after meeting Ned and Joe. Li Chen, of course, went to the meeting with three other members of the *zhenying*, even though he knew that his sister was opposed to a violent rebellion.

When they returned, Li Chen gave Li Ping some of the basic details about what was planned – nothing more. He told her that Ned Kelly had written a Declaration of Independence which included citizens' rights for all people, including Chinese, and a promise to abolish the residents' tax.

'We'll be free, finally', he told her.

Li Ping asked with great firmness how and when this would happen. She knew that, although he might not tell her the full truth, he would not lie either.

'We'll join an army of supporters, just like the farmers of Sanyuanli', he said. 'We'll wait in the bush at Glenrowan. The Kelly gang will derail a train carrying police and troopers, bail them up and take their weapons. After I hear three rapid shots, I'll fire skyrockets from the bush and our army will move in to take the police and troopers prisoner. Small groups of the army will then rob banks in Benalla and Beechworth to make a treasury for us all.'

He continued, 'Ned will declare independence and the prisoners will be kept hostage while he negotiates with the government for our freedom and secures the release of his mother and other prisoners in Beechworth'.

Li Ping looked grave. What she said surprised and frightened Li Chen.

'My Brother, perhaps we won't have long before the police come after us and our friends. I know they're putting up "Wanted" posters in Chinese all over the Woolshed, Beechworth and other places as well. How can we be sure no one will speak just to get money? How can we be sure Fook Shing will not betray us? Changes are coming, dear Brother, and they may not be favourable. You must be fully aware of the dangers we face. True liberation depends on this deep awareness. It is not too late to alter course. What's in your heart right now, my Brother?'

She did not get a direct reply, just the simple words, 'There is much to do'.

As the years passed, Li Ping often wondered about the time between this last conversation with her brother and the terrible events at Glenrowan. Could she have done more to avert the violent death of Joe and Li Chen's disintegration into madness? Li Ping's heart moved towards a great silence.

Just one episode, which lasted only an hour or so, returned to her in dreams and in moments of solitude for the rest of her life.

It took place on the night before the battle at Glenrowan when a frantic, breathless Joe arrived around midnight at her hut in the Chinese camp. He told her that he had just shot and killed Aaron Sherritt and begged her to let him stay with her for a while. She lit a candle on her altar beside her bed. It flickered beneath his face and Guanyin.

'Yes, Ah Joe, you can sit beside me here', she said, sitting on her bed.

In the warm smoky light of the candle, she saw his ruptured heart open and then close so tightly that she could no longer properly recognise him.

As his heart opened, a child was conceived.

〜

It was Ah Fuey who broke the news to Li Ping about the killing at Glenrowan. His face, scratched and bloodied from riding fast through thick bush, was contorted with the agony of his words.

'It was a disaster', he told her. 'Nothing went to plan. The rockets were fired at the wrong time. Everyone was confused about what to do. Li Chen went into a rage and ran towards the gunfight but, when no one followed him, he ran back. There were many gunshots. As each one sounded, Li Chen shook like he had been shot himself and waved his arms about madly till he fell on to the ground, crying. He cried for a long time. I don't know how long. We couldn't console him. When he did stop, it was as though he had turned into stone and wood.'

'I'm sorry, Li Ping. We're all sorry.'

'Ah Fuey, may I ask, where he is now?'

'Some of the Europeans put him in a cart. Pensang Zi got in with him and they went straight to the asylum called Mayday. It's on the other side of Beechworth near Little Guangzhou. They're still there, I think.'

'Thank you, Ah Fuey. And what happened to the Kelly men and Ah Joe?'

The distressed man took a deep and uneasy breath. Looking at the ground, he said, 'Ned Kelly is wounded. He was shot many times by the police. All the others are dead. All dead.'

Li Ping brought her hands together and bowed to Ah Fuey. She remained silent as her tears flowed and she began a slow walk to Mrs Byrne's place.

A few minutes later, the two women stood facing each other, Li Ping still crying silently, while Mrs Byrne, leaning on a pitchfork, kept her jaw clenched. 'He left me years ago', she told Li Ping. 'And now, he'll never return. So be it. I will not be seeking the return of his body. I've got more important things to do with the little money I've got, like feeding his sisters.'

Li Ping was not surprised by Mrs Byrne's reaction, but wished this strong Irish woman would put her arms around her. She wanted to smell the skin of a Byrne again.

'Mrs Byrne, perhaps we can eat together this evening after I return from visiting my brother at the asylum. I can bring corn soup.'

'All right. Thank you.'

∽

It took more than three hours for Li Ping to walk to Mayday. She followed Reedy Creek up the valley to its source at the waterfalls and climbed over wet rocks and boulders to reach the main road into town. Once she was on the public carriageway, the walking became easier, but her anxiety intensified with every step, all the way to the front doors of the asylum.

Li Ping thought Mayday looked like a palace with its white three-storey walls and its colonnaded entrance. However, as she entered, she was overwhelmed by the smell of bleach and the moans echoing through the panelled corridors.

A nurse approached her quickly and aggressively. 'What are you doing here?' she demanded.

'Thank you, Missus. I wish to see my brother, Li Chen, who was brought here yesterday.'

'I'll see if that is possible, but I must tell you only one visit is permitted each week.'

Li Ping waited in the grand vestibule. She sat down on a long wooden bench and her stomach clenched. Dropping her head between her knees, she held off the impulse to vomit as she cried on to the mosaic floor.

The nurse's heavy boots echoed through corridors as she returned to the vestibule.

'Come this way.'

Li Ping had never been in such a building and struggled to keep up with the nurse who piloted her through passageway after passageway. Every door was closed and from behind each one came some type of wailing. This is a cauldron, she thought.

They stopped beside an opening in the wall. Neither a door nor a window, just a gap in the masonry with two wooden shutters, one on top of the other. The nurse removed the top shutter. It took time for Li Ping's eyes to adjust but gradually her brother came into view, sitting on a bed with his arms bound around him in a type of canvas jacket that Li Ping had never seen before. Despite the noisy clattering as the nurse removed the shutter, Li Chen did not turn his head toward the opening where his sister stood.

'Beloved Brother', she called softly. 'It's me, Li Ping.'

Li Chen made no movement or sound.

She called again. Louder this time. But still no response.

'He has not spoken since he arrived', said the nurse whose name she told Li Ping was Sister Hilda. 'He was violent at first, which is why we had to put him in a straitjacket. He could have hurt someone. Do you understand?'

'Yes, I do', she said. 'I have seen his rages, but …'

Sister Hilda put her hand consolingly but formally on Li Ping's shoulder and said quietly, 'We might be able to take it off in a little while if he remains calm'.

'Thank you, Sister.'

Li Ping called to him again and again, but he did not react.

'Please, Sister, can I sit with him?'

'No. Certainly not', the nurse said. 'We'll see if there's any change, though the doctor doesn't think it likely. You must prepare yourself. He may never recover.'

And, with that, Sister Hilda locked the shutter back into position and Li Ping commenced the long walk home.

The following morning, Li Ping took her usual path at her usual time to the little tin temple. It was a weary walk after waking feeling heavy from a night of gruesome dreams, about which, thankfully, she had lost all details.

The ducks were up and about as she expected, but there was nobody on the paths – not a single person making their way to work or doing morning exercises. After news about Glenrowan travelled through the camp, despair and panic sent everyone into hiding. Some feared arrest for being in the bush during the siege. Others felt that any chance of a fairer life in *Tsin Chin Shan* was gone forever. For Li Ping, the aftermath of extreme violence, although she had not witnessed it, made her feel like she was drowning alone.

In the temple, her mind became agitated and unfocused. Random thoughts turned from images of Li Chen in his canvas bindings to Joe's softest touches, Guanyin's mercy for all, the hell of raining bullets, lifeless bodies still bleeding into the dust, the first radishes. And so it went, on and on. She thought of the *yueqin* lying on Li Chen's bed in their hut: the way Li Chen brought it to life, the way it brought him to life. Then, finally, after more than an hour of unbroken despair, she thought that there was something positive she could do: she could take Li Chen's *yueqin* to him.

On the morning of the seventh day after her first visit, Li Ping wrapped the *yueqin* in Li Chen's winter jacket and slid it into his knapsack. She packed two moon cakes and a bowl of rice with dried fish as well. The knapsack, with the protruding neck of the *yueqin*, made the climb near the waterfall a risky route. So, caught between mourning and hope, Li Ping walked the long way through the valley into town, then out the eastern side and up the hill where the white asylum overlooked the entire settlement.

Just after midday, she stepped under the portico and into the vestibule where the tile floors were wet with bleach and ammonia, the smell causing her to gag. She sat on the bench, trying to steady herself in the intolerable atmosphere. She felt as though her skin and lungs were rejecting her being in this place.

Sister Hilda arrived and escorted her through the same passageways where every sound, step, shadow and spoken word was a repeat of her first visit. Li Chen looked unchanged too. He sat on his bed in a straitjacket staring at the opposite wall, unmoved by the sound of the shutter coming down and Li Ping calling his name. Stepping back, Li Ping looked at her brother framed by the opening in the blank white wall like a painted figure in a dark picture.

'Sister Hilda, why is he still bound like that? Can you please release his arms so he can hold his *yueqin*?'

'That's a decision for the doctor. I'll ask next time he visits. You can leave the instrument with me.'

'Thank you, Sister, but I'll keep it until I can hand it to him. Perhaps next week?'

'Perhaps.'

Once more, Li Ping stepped her way home for the routines of another week before she could visit again. Sameness was not a cause for boredom or anxiety for Li Ping. It provided a stillness in the chaos of the world of objects, a stillness slowly absorbing her grief for Li Chen and her longing for Joe.

She decided to walk through Mrs Byrne's farm on the way home since they had not seen each other for a few days. When they met earlier in the week, Mrs Byrne seemed remote and downcast. While weeding the house garden together, she said, 'I will not make room in my heart for him. I will not.'

To Li Ping, Mrs Byrne's statement seemed an expression of hope that one day she may no longer even remember him and so be cleansed of him.

The thought saddened her. She wished to be able to recall every detail of her Ah Joe forever: the milkiness of his skin, the traces of Music, the smell of whisky, the rhythm of his Cantonese … and the speeding of his heart when he had been so close to her for that moment which would never recur.

Yes', she thought. 'I will not forget a single moment of Ah Joe.'

Li Ping would confide that truth to her Bodhisattva again and again for the rest of her life.

∽

As Li Ping drew closer to the farm, she hoped that Mrs Byrne might invite her in. Perhaps a conversation would allow them to reveal their mutual love for Joe? Perhaps such a conversation would create a deeper bond between her son's lover and his mother?

However, Mrs Byrne and her children were nowhere to be seen that afternoon. At least there was washing on the line. Li Ping felt relieved, thinking that they would not have gone far.

∽

The third trip to Mayday revealed a change in Li Chen's condition. Li Ping was not taken through the long passages but escorted down a short corridor to what Sister Hilda called 'the airing yard'.

'Please, Sister, what is the airing yard?'

'It's where we take patients to get fresh air and we wash them down with hoses if they've soiled themselves.'

The nurse opened one of the two french doors at the end of the corridor from which they stepped out into a perfectly square, stone-paved quadrangle formed by the high white masonry walls of the asylum. Four or five inmates sat on separate steel benches around the perimeter and Li Ping was delighted to see Li Chen unbound and sitting against the south wall.

She removed his *yueqin* from the knapsack and approached slowly, as if about to pick up an injured animal or bird. He didn't recognise her. Perhaps he cannot see me at all, she thought, trying to settle herself within his vacant gaze. She sat beside him whispering his name and, when she plucked one of the strings of the *yueqin*, he breathed a deeper breath. Placing his beloved instrument across his knees, she lifted his left hand toward the neck, opened his fist and closed his fingers gently across the strings. She held out the bone pick found on the deck of the *Land O'Cakes* and he took it between his thumb and forefinger. They sat together motionless for a moment of calm and then, with slow soft movements, he played the first tune which he had played all those years ago in the kitchen of their house in Guangzhou.

Li Ping's heart was full again. She whispered, 'Brother, that is beautiful'.

Li Chen's expression did not change. He made no verbal reply, but played the tune again from the beginning, a little louder this time.

Sister Hilda, standing by the doorway, smiled and indicated to Li Ping that it was time for her to leave. As they walked together toward the portico, the nurse said, 'I've never seen anything like that before, especially with catatonic inmates'.

'Please, Sister, what is "catatonic"?'

'Some people, like your brother, who've experienced a terrible shock, can never fully engage again with the world that delivered them such horror. The doctor is certain he'll never speak again, but his music is very positive. You're a very good sister.'

~

When the day for the fourth visit to Mayday came around, Li Ping woke feeling sick in the stomach for the third or fourth morning in a row. She vomited, then packed the knapsack with some food and water and set off via the waterfall track. It was a struggle, and she dry-retched after reaching the top of the boulder hills.

When she reached Mayday, Sister Hilda met her at the front door under the portico.

'Your brother is walking in the gardens with an

orderly. They've gone that way', said the nurse, pointing toward the path that wound its way to the north.

Beautiful trees grew in the grounds of Mayday and beside the pathway, garden beds with marigolds ran all the way to the cream and brown octagonal rotunda where Li Ping could see her brother sitting. The orderly stood outside, like a sentry.

Li Ping sat beside Li Chen and quietly said, 'Good morning, Brother', but nothing else, not wanting to risk causing him agitation. She was not certain if he knew she was there but felt that her quiet presence would do little harm.

After nearly an hour of sitting in silence under the rotunda, the orderly moved in and took Li Chen gently by the arm. He showed no resistance and Li Ping walked with them to the portico, and, when they went inside, she commenced her journey home.

Li Ping stopped regularly on her way home. She felt depleted by her stomach sickness and her brother's condition. On top of the waterfall, she ate a pear and sat beside the rock pool feeding the stream of water running over the edge and down the valley in a mighty rush. She stretched out on the warm rocks lying face down, her hands in the cool stream. She observed her reflection which struggled to offer kindness. She was looking directly at her agony and fear.

Plunging her face through her reflection as deep into the pool at it would go, she held herself there. Then, raising her head, gasping, she repeated the movements until it was all over. Exactly what 'it' was, she did not know – perhaps a cleansing – but she could now walk more easily and decided to call into Mrs Byrne's place on the way.

⁓

Smoke coming from the chimney lifted Li Ping's spirits. Mrs Byrne might be baking biscuits, she thought. Perhaps I'm not eating enough, she wondered.

Sure enough, Mrs Byrne was there and very pleased to see her. She made tea without milk for her Celestial neighbour and produced a plate of the heartiest oat cakes that Li Ping had ever tasted.

'You're a very hungry woman today, Li Ping', she said.

'Yes, Missus, I am. I've been very sick every morning for the last three or four days. No appetite most of the day and then I get very hungry later in the evening.'

Mrs Byrne stopped still in the middle of the kitchen.

'Li Ping, I have a very personal question to ask you. Are your breasts feeling tender?'

'Yes, Missus. I noticed that when I lay on the rock at the waterfall.'

'Jesus, Mary and Joseph!' Mrs Byrne cried. 'Li Ping, you are with child … Good grief! … and I know who the father must be.'

The Mirror Itself

The tough, Irish dairy widow told Li Ping that she was not able to deal with any more dependents and the Chinese camp was no place for a woman bearing the 'half-caste child of a murderer'. She suggested Li Ping might be able to live permanently on a vast pastoral estate, Donnally Downs, in the southwest, owned by Daman Donnally and his wife Brenna, Margaret Byrne's second cousin.

'She's the green sheep of the family', said Mrs Byrne with a laugh and a snarl. 'But a good woman all the same. A woman of charity. I'll tell you all about her on our journey.'

Li Ping realised that Mrs Byrne would be changing her life forever by removing her from the gardens and the valley. The Irish dairy farmer was certainly intent on separating her from her brother, who she saw as a malignant presence. Nevertheless, Li Ping felt a deep obligation to Li Chen even though he didn't respond to her at all. His protection and his music had made her life bearable for so many years. Yet she had an overwhelming duty to her unborn and an additional duty to all who gave rise to the expanding life within her.

'And what is this additional duty, really?' she asked herself over and over as she sat in the octagonal pavilion where she once taught Joe Byrne her language. She cried when she remembered seeing him again at the garden gate and more tears fell when she remembered sitting close to Li Chen on the cart on the way back from the opera singing 'Agony in Autumn'. She did not wish for time to close over memories but, as she allowed the reality of the present day itself to overtake thoughts of the past, her stability began to return.

'My duty is to my practice with Guanyin. Without that, my child has no chance for the liberation Li Chen and Ah Joe were seeking but with such delusions.' This realisation became her mantra, her guide for her own life and that of the child within her, the seed of Joe Byrne, writer, linguist, son, horseman, lover, gangster, compatriot, romantic, bushman, singer and murderer.

It was a Saturday morning in the spring of 1880 when Li Ping and Margaret Byrne boarded the steam train at Beechworth Station for Melbourne on the first leg of a journey through the richest city on earth and then on to Geelong. From there, westward to the upper reaches of the Barwon River.

Li Ping had never seen a steam locomotive before at such close quarters. From a distance, the machines always made her think of a dragon caterpillar scurrying through the trees but, up close, the enormity of its wheels, rods and bolts made her shudder. It seemed such an angry, wheezing beast. No wonder people call it the 'iron horse', she thought. But as she walked on to the platform and saw its giant bulging shape, she gasped, 'How could men on horses think they could challenge this?'

Climbing aboard with her two hessian bags and the pole which had been with her since leaving Guangzhou, she hesitated before entering the carriage. She said to herself but with her lips moving slightly, 'This is what they planned to attack. They were ready to sacrifice

everyone on board. What of the old people and children, or pregnant women like me who would be widowed and fatherless?' She clutched her belly to calm herself and to protect that part of Joe growing inside her.

Li Ping could hear Mrs Byrne huffing behind her. Pulling herself up from the platform and cutting through Li Ping's thoughts, she said, 'Don't just stand there. Go inside.' Which she did and found, to her delight, a ruby-painted, timber-panelled carriage with brass lamps and

luggage racks. The green leather seat covers were fastened around their edges by brass tacks with little domed heads glinting in the sun that was shining through the square windows down each side of the carriage. Li Ping saw them as jewels.

'Keep moving, Li Ping. Go to the front of the carriage', Mrs Byrne instructed, lumping her suitcase which also contained Li Ping's tea pot, a small wok and incense sticks. In her own bag, Mrs Byrne had carefully stowed the Chinese vase, 'Demon' Donnally's gift on the birth of Joe.

With some heft, Mrs Byrne got their luggage on to the overhead racks and the two women sat close to each other looking silently across the carriage, through the windows and out to the railway yards. Beyond, they could see smoke rising from cooking fires in Beechworth's Little Guangzhou – Li Ping's first home in the town where she had now spent most of her life.

As the iron beast snorted lumps of soot into the air, its tail shuddered, jolting the women from side to side. Li Ping gripped the edge of her seat. Her fingertips found the smooth domed heads of the tacks hemming the seats. She was calmed by their feel as the carriage rocked and rattled down the tracks towards Melbourne.

For ages, the women just sat, acclimatising themselves to the uncommon motion and the gnashing thwack of metal, glass, leather and wood in the hinged assembly propelling itself faster than any horse and buggy. They were both alarmed and thrilled by the experience, the rhythmic clacking of wheels on rail joints both exciting and lulling.

Mrs Byrne scanned the carriage and saw that there were only six other passengers on board. A couple, and a group of four who immediately opened newspapers.

How can they possibly read on this thing, she wondered?

Nevertheless, Mrs Byrne was relieved that she would not be overheard when talking to Li Ping about where they were going and the family conflicts which had set her and her cousin apart. She felt a familiar core of resentment beginning to burn as she thought about where to start. Finally, without looking at Li Ping, she just blurted:

'My cousin married a rich old Protestant, Daman Donnally, about forty years ago. "Demon" Donnally he's called, but don't you use that name. Be hell to pay. Anyway, Brenna was a housemaid and barmaid at the Cornwall Hotel in Launceston, in old Van Diemen's Land where he lived temporarily. Apparently, he came from India and was in China working for that big English trading company. I've forgotten its name.'

'The East India Company?' Li Ping recalled her father railing against the company which was a major exporter of opium to the Celestial Kingdom. 'My father said they were murders. They had their own army in my country.'

'I'm not surprised. Yes, East India, that's the one. The

story goes that, after the first Mrs Donnally died on the voyage to Van Diemen's Land, he took up with my cousin not long after he landed. Don't know whether the wife was buried at sea or on land after he arrived. But I've always wondered what he thought when he first heard my cousin's Galway accent. I mean, he's a real Protestant, a bit extreme and not very fond of Catholics, so maybe she disguised it? She was always the canny one with an eye for the main chance. Maybe he didn't care? Maybe she faked a proddy-dog accent? Maybe they didn't do much talking? Not at bedtime anyway', she winked to Li Ping, 'Mmmm – that would be right'. Mrs Byrne laughed grimly.

Li Ping could not easily interpret that wink. She was thinking about antagonism between Catholics and Protestants. She would do everything she could not to take sides. Guanyin did not permit her to support anger and violence, the violence that killed Ah Joe and the violence which Ah Joe used to kill his best friend. The events of Glenrowan and the cruelty of the strongly Protestant colonial government confirmed her sympathy for the victimised Catholics, but she would have no part in their endless sectarian warring.

The dairy-farming Catholic mother of six maintained a fixed gaze on the paddocks and trees whizzing by and continued her story. 'He had plenty of cash with him as well as trunks of flash vases, pieces of art and crates of furniture collected while travelling around India and

China. Apparently, he was an actuary, some sort of accountant inspecting cargo heading back to England. The choice pieces were his for the taking. Not that I'm saying he was a thief, Li Ping, but there was all that finery just a touch away. You know that vase on my table? It was his present to me when Joe was born. Very old, beautiful thing. You know it?'

'Yes, I remember. I think it might be from the time of the Ming Dynasty.'

Li Ping knew the provenance of the vase. She wondered if it could have been taken by the British after the bombardment of Guangzhou. So many houses and great public buildings like libraries and civic offices were destroyed or wrecked. Perhaps the British officers took them as prizes for themselves, or to sell to those who were enchanted by the objects of the Celestial Kingdom but not its people?

At this point, Margaret Byrne realised that she had been mostly talking to herself, though the pregnant Chinese woman had been listening carefully. This was already one of the longest periods they had spent together, and Mrs Byrne's tears nearly surfaced as she considered her lot compared to the luxury which her cousin enjoyed.

'It's not that they're rich, and I'm poor. It's how they got rich that I can't abide – just packed up and joined a bunch of rich Protestants and sailed into Port Phillip. No right to be there, but somehow they found a huge area of land and just stayed. So easy! Squatters! We called them "squatters" – people who paid nothing for the land, cleared it illegally and made fortunes. New Wool Mountain, they should call this place. Sheep will never be mined out. There's a saying, Li Ping: "All that glitters is not gold". That's certainly true of the wool fleece. Mark my words. What the squatters did was illegal but, there you are, they got away with it.'

'But if I break the law now, or even then, I'd end up in jail – probably with hard labour. Just look how the law came down on Joe and his mates for taking a cow or a horse. But Donnally and his make-believe Protestant wife, they took thousands of acres for themselves – as much, they say, as all of Dublin. And not one person raised a finger. They made the law to suit themselves.'

'Ah well. Good on them, I suppose. They lived hard for years with convicts and blacks till they got their deals done with the Land Commissioner for proper title. Then they built the homestead and the fences and now they have their own world: workers, servants, gardens and more sheep than anyone can count. There's a village of shearers' quarters, workers' huts, sheds and stables. Even a school and their own chapel.'

'Which reminds me. We'll arrive on Sunday and my cousin's not too happy about that because Sunday's "the day of rest" and she polices it like a trooper. No worker's allowed to pick up a shovel or ride a horse and even the servants are sent to their quarters after preparing a cold lunch. Everyone must attend chapel for a bible reading either at dawn or at sunset, preferably both.'

Li Ping shifted a little closer to Mrs Byrne and asked quietly, 'Do they pray together?'

What a question, pondered Mrs Byrne.

'Of course ... Well, I think so. I've only been once. Yes, I think so', she replied, still surprised by what interested Li Ping.

'Brenna has become quite the lay preacher with a bit of a County Kerry accent like that of "The Demon" ... and for Jesus' sake, make sure you don't call him that.'

'I'm told he has a huge library. My cousin spent so much time reading, she made herself the schoolteacher for both her children and those of the servants and labourers. She did it for years, until recently. Now they're so rich, they've hired a teacher from Ireland. I wonder what Joe would be now, if he'd been born into an educated family like my cousin and her husband have produced?'

'What do you mean, Mrs Byrne?'

The older woman turned and looked directly at Li Ping. At first glance, Margaret Byrne thought that Li Ping's face was expressionless till she saw her eyes conveying something unbearable for both of them.

And the train steamed on, passing through cuttings and broad farm acres. When it stopped at sidings for water and coal, the women sipped cold black tea and ate rice cakes which Li Ping had made for the journey. They arrived in Melbourne later than expected and managed to board the last train to Geelong just in time. They slept most of the way, leaning against each other. Li Ping had grown used to the sour milk smell of Europeans, including Mrs Byrne, but was grateful for the sprig of lavender pinned to Mrs Byrne's bonnet.

It was nearly dark when they arrived in Geelong and, with the permission of the station master, the women found a space on the floor of the waiting room to spend the night. As they lay down on their bed rolls, Li Ping asked, 'Why will your cousin have me?'

'As I said, my cousin and her family are good people. They believe their wealth means they should help people, that they're doing God's work with what God has given them. I won't quarrel with that, but I still think they took what wasn't theirs … though perhaps it was a kind of gift as well.'

'In any case, they believe in charity', she went on. 'I can't do what they'll do for you, Li Ping, but I'm sure you'll gratefully accept what they offer. I just wish I could provide the same. But I'll pay them some rent, give them something for taking you and your baby off me hands. It would be good', she continued, somewhat bitterly, 'if none of us needed them … or their charity or their church.'

She paused, sighed and said to Li Ping, 'Time for sleep now. Tomorrow you'll have a safe new home.'

At seven o'clock they boarded the Cobb & Co. Royal Mail coach to Hamilton, which had a scheduled stop at the roadside delivery for Donnally Downs by about five in the afternoon. Brenna Donnally had purchased two of the more expensive inside seats for the women, who were both grateful not to be travelling on the outside seats, or up on the roof with the luggage. Fifteen people in all – plus driver, luggage and mail – were aboard when the five-horse team pulled away for its first stop at Germantown on the outskirts of Geelong, the biggest wool port in the colony.

The motion and sounds of the coach were so different to the train. The smell of horse and harness was homely and much preferred by both women to the stinking firebox and screeching wheels of the train. Once again, the women slept leaning on each other, shoulder to shoulder. Through her sleep, Margaret Byrne could hear passengers muttering about why Chinese were allowed inside the coach.

'Unheard of – there should be a law', said a well-dressed elderly woman with a strained English accent.

'I think there is', hissed her female Scots companion while stabbing the floor of the coach with her parasol.

Margaret Byrne was about to give them a piece of her mind when they arrived in Germantown, and the brittle, pinched-looking pair alighted. 'They are all Protestants around here', snorted Mrs Byrne.

Standing at the grand bluestone entrance pillars and archway of Donnally Downs, luggage at her feet and stagecoach dust settling around her, Li Ping felt that she was deep inside a dream. Two days of travelling had left her with no bearings and no sense of regular time. Standing still, for the first time since leaving Beechworth, she clearly felt the movement of her unborn child. She also felt a sense of escape after being released from the chaos of Li Chen's insanity and the loom of the decades of conflict which riddled the struggles on the gold diggings.

Li Ping had the feeling of immanent disappearance as well. Her thoughts and feelings returned to the bombardment of her home and the sanctuary of the nunnery. She remembered how the Great Bell rang involuntarily as the shells landed nearby and recalled the feeling of safety in isolation. She chanted silently:

Gaté gaté pāragate pārasamgate bodhi svāhā
Gone, gone, gone beyond, gone fully beyond,
Awakened now!

'This way', called Mrs Byrne standing beside the mail delivery bin with a piece of paper in her hand.

'My cousin says, if we arrive around 5 pm, we should walk up past the homestead and around the back to the chapel, which is next to the vegetable garden. They'll be having bible reading at 6 pm.'

Mrs Byrne was tired and grumpy at the prospect of a mile-long walk with a case. 'They could have left a horse and buggy for us down here', she muttered toward the ground as she took her first steps.

Li Ping squatted deeply to thread her hessian bags on to her pole. With a little balancing shrug, she hoisted her load evenly across her shoulders and, within a few steps, found the comfortable rhythm that had taken her from Robe to Ararat a quarter of a century ago.

It was a nearly effortless walk for her up this tree-lined, winding driveway that she had never seen before. The trees were evenly spaced and well rooted in thick grass. Coming out of the final bend in the road, Li Ping saw the bluestone homestead just beyond a wide, circular driveway glinting with white quartz. A rose garden blooming in red and yellow welcomed the new arrivals through an entrance bower and pergola.

She walked ahead of Mrs Byrne, even though she had no clear idea about where to go. She stopped, waiting in the fragrant shade of the climbing blooms, thankful for the most auspicious colours of her childhood to be around her. It didn't take long for the older woman to catch up, despite her suitcase. They rested briefly under the pergola before Mrs Byrne, in a much easier mood, led the way, motioning Li Ping to follow.

The low, wide bluestone homestead with its white veranda posts and window casements came into clear view. They crossed the quartz path circling to the right, past wicker chairs with sleeping cats and through another bower of climbing roses where a series of lily ponds trickled into each other along the east side of the house. Ahead was an iron gate set within an archway cut through a hedge. Passing through the gate, a bluestone path lay between rows of vegetable beds. Li Ping smiled at the young seedlings in the early days of their growth cycle, readying for the summer harvest.

As the two women passed through the last gate and headed toward the little weatherboard building with its steep roof and a small portico over the front door, Li Ping recalled the monasteries of her youth. She saw again their ordered internal and external spaces, each with its own threshold and each with a path to another point of arrival.

Mrs Byrne pointed to the cross at the apex of the iron roof.

'That's the chapel. Put your bags down here under the portico and follow me inside.'

She was grumpy again, feeling manipulated into a Protestant service where everyone would disapprove if she crossed herself thus revealing her faith and lower-class origin. Being of the Catholic faith implied, she knew, stupidity to these self-satisfied burghers, even if one was her own cousin.

Damn them, she said to herself as she ushered Li Ping into the back row of the austere little place of compulsory devotion.

The only face that Li Ping could see through the heads and shoulders of perhaps fifteen men and women was that of Brenna Donnally, a tall, big-boned, broad-jawed woman who read with authority and well-rehearsed admonishment.

'I read now from Matthew, Chapter 12, on The Law of the Sabbath, Verses 30 to 32.'

> *30 He that is not with me is against me; and he that gathereth not with me scattereth abroad.*
>
> *31 Wherefore I say unto you, All manner of sin and blasphemy shall be forgiven unto men: but the blasphemy against the Holy Ghost shall not be forgiven unto men.*
>
> *32 And whosoever speaketh a word against the Son of man, it shall be forgiven him: but whosoever speaketh against the Holy Ghost, it shall not be forgiven him, neither in this world, neither in the world to come.*

'Here endeth the lesson. Thank you for your attendance. Continue your day of rest in the presence of Jesus Our Saviour, for tomorrow is a new day and the beginning of a new week of righteous toil in the name of the Lord.'

Li Ping and Margaret Byrne remained seated as the

servants and workers filed out into the cool dusk. Mrs Byrne, looking toward the simple wooden cross on the lace-covered table, stood slowly and crossed herself as her cousin closed the bible on the lectern. Brenna Donnally did not react to her cousin's religious gesture but simply placed the sacred book on the table and walked briskly toward the new arrivals.

'Welcome, cousin', she said, offering her hand rather than an embrace.

'This must be Li Ping. Welcome, my dear. Did you understand the bible reading?'

Li Ping brought her palms together and bowed, 'Thank you, madam. I understood a little.'

'What did you understand?'

'That forgiveness is possible for everything except denial of our Buddha nature. If we deny it, we can never be it.'

Mrs Brenna Donnally, having confidence in her faith and social standing, was taken aback.

'Very good. But, in future, please only refer to Jesus in this place. You are, however, free to conduct your Buddhistic beliefs in your own quarters. I understand you believe in sobriety and compassion. That's a very good start. We'll get along very well, I'm sure. And now, you two weary travellers, I'll show you to your quarters.'

As they set off in the falling light, an old man with a powerful voice called out from behind them.

'Brenna! Brenna! Great news just came in on the

telegraph. The government's ignored that petition not to execute Ned Kelly. Could you believe more than thirty thousand idiots in the colony signed it? It got them nowhere; the murderous fool was hanged this morning. Good riddance. One less Catholic Irishman.'

Brenna Donnally quietly contemplated her own ethnicity and Christian compassion as she led them past the chapel, between the stables and the vegetable garden. Li Ping saw a small cottage with slab walls and a window each side of a central door. The low veranda, she thought, looked like an eye lid. Perhaps it is watching them?

Mrs Donnally pushed open a creaky door, lit a lamp beside the chimney and, as the amber light expanded across the single room, said, 'There's only one bed but there's a bed roll in the corner by the basin. Get some sleep and we'll breakfast together in the morning.'

'Just a minute, Brenna. I have something for you, something I know Joe would like you to have for, for – uh, as it were – rent.'

'What's this, Margaret? You know we don't need money. It's our duty and will be a pleasure …'

From her bag Margaret Byrne took the vase, 'I'm simply returning it, returning it to you and your husband who gave it to me when my son Joe was born.'

Brenna held the vase, looked it over, touching the rim.

'Yes, I do remember it. Very beautiful but …'

'Take it, Brenna, take it. He has no use for a vase.

And I have no use for the memories', she said with a toughness that Li Ping wished she could soften.

As Mrs Donnally closed the door behind her, the two women looked at each other in silence. The news of Ned's execution and the manner of Daman Donnally's announcement had so infuriated Mrs Byrne that she could hardly speak – partly for fear of being overheard by her relative and partly because of her decision not to accept her son's body or attend his burial.

She would not and could not summon up any feelings for the last of the men who had made her life so hard for so many years. Nevertheless, she had admired Kelly and his cause and was secretly proud of her son's allegiance to Ned and his ambitions.

Li Ping sat on the edge of the bed silently, following her breathing as it shuddered from the pit of her stomach.

Finally, Mrs Byrne put her hands on her hips and thrust her head forward.

'Murderer, yes. Fool, no. I cannot break bread with them. My work here is done.'

Mrs Byrne threw her suitcase on to the bed beside Li Ping, wrestled the straps open with shaking hands and pulled out the wok, the tea pot and the incense. Closing her case, she stared at Li Ping.

'Sorry, but you'll be safe here. Me and my kind are not.'

Li Ping had seen Mrs Byrne angry before but only with her children and the police. That was nothing like the fury now driving her out into the night alone. As Li Ping tried to balance herself after the tumult of a long day unlike any other, she wept. Seeing her misery, Mrs Byrne took half a step towards her but, thinking better of it, muttered a goodbye, wished her well and headed down the driveway in search of a lift to the nearest town.

∽

Li Ping had arrived at the great property wearing her long working tunic and loose pants. Mrs Donnally loved the knot buttons and loops fastening the tunic around her neck and closing the sleeves around her wrists. She told the mother-to-be that Chinese clothes suited her and that she must always wear them.

When the newborn arrived seven months later, Li Ping dressed her in garments of the same fabric as her own clothes. Brenna Donnally, the matriarch of the great property, called the baby 'Little Li' and, over the years, always loved seeing her little doll, Li Ping, and the doll's doll, her child, making their way through the garden to commence their duties in the homestead. Year after year, they left their cottage just beyond the house garden and walked the flagstone path to the back door together. They were a pair, always a pair, in their identical loose clothes.

Li Ping's duties included dusting throughout the wide, flat house with its heavy verandas, especially the dark formal rooms with fine furniture and objects from all quadrants of the empire. Since her arrival, Mrs Donnally's interest in Chinese objects of all kinds had led her to turn a spare bedroom into 'The Canton Room', as she called it. Silk and gold tapestries and scrolls hung on the walls, and blue and white vases, nearly as tall as Li Ping, stood in the doorway. Green and white jade carvings of all sizes sat on black lacquered sideboards and tables. Li Ping often wondered if any of the objects had taken their final form in Li Chen's hands.

Mrs Donnally imported traditional formal clothing for mother and child. But not the close-fitting *chèuhngsāam qipao*, which seemed too lewd and would encourage too much attention from the workers. She preferred the straight lines and drape of the *chángpáo*, especially when made from deep blue silk. It never occurred to her that she was creating a uniform for the mother and child. Her heart had returned to her own childhood and her toys and dolls. And now, she had Li Ping and Little Li.

Occasionally, when the men spent days away on distant parts of the run, Li Ping performed a tea ceremony in The Canton Room. The big Irish woman's place in one of the four hand-carved, rosewood *huanhuali* 黄花梨 chairs was the northern-most one. Li Ping was invited to take the western chair and her child, the southern one. The eastern chair was always left empty – a pleasing sight for Li Ping, who was calmed by its emptiness. At other times she would fill the chair herself with memories of Li Chen, her mother or father. And sometimes Ah Joe.

Mrs Donnally watched Li Ping's every movement as she began the ritual on the round jade inlaid table in the centre of the chairs of the four directions. First, warming the cups and tea pot with hot water from the thick-walled ceramic jug and then discarding it slowly into the tray with its bamboo grate and well.

She marvelled at the ease with which mother and child remained silent and watched closely each of Li Ping's movements as the hot water was poured over the imported leaves. Every step was defined by stillness – even the action of sipping from the tiny cups which Mrs Donnally thought of as thimbles.

≈

Steadily, year by year, the Donnallys fulfilled their promise of protection for mother and child by separating them from everyone on the property and the world beyond.

Mrs Donnally had barely noticed the child growing up and the gradual emergence of features common to her own country of origin.

One day during a tea ceremony, this slow change became obvious to both women. Li Ping noticed that Mrs Donnally's attention was more on the child than the ceremony. And the Irish lady of the house realised, for the first time, that the child's hair was becoming wavy and ever so slightly red. A shaft of midday sun reflected from the veranda into the grey-blue eyes of the five-year-old China doll. Just for an instant, but long enough for

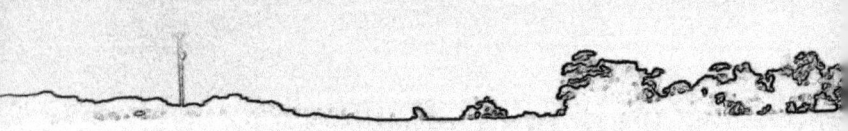

Mrs Donnally to be reminded of how this mother and child came to be with her.

A sense of unease engulfed her. The undeniably sweet baby was taking the form of a half-caste who had no place anywhere. Perhaps not even on this property. Mrs Donnally's thoughts turned to the years ahead, after the eventual death of Li Ping. She gulped her tea and brought the ceremony to a close. Li Ping realised then that her child was a stranger unlike any other.

⌣

Soon after, when Little Li was about seven years old, she started at the school on Donnally Downs and one day after school asked her mother about her father. Li Ping, surprised, simply said, 'He was an Irishman who loved music and horses. Sadly, he died before you were born. I'll tell you more, but he was a man who had many feelings in his heart.'

'Good feelings?'

'Yes, good feelings.'

'Bad feelings?'

'Some bad as well. Now, get on with helping me with the wood, Little Li. It's getting late. Less talking, please.'

Little Li often wondered when her mother would tell her more about her father but felt hesitant to ask again. However, one evening after finishing a stew of swede and parsnip, Little Li asked, 'What was my father's name?'

'Ah Joe', Li Ping replied. 'He was happiest when riding his horse Music and speaking Cantonese.'

'How did he learn our language, Mother?'

'He had many friends from where I was born. And I taught him a little. He was a very fast learner. It was nice to be with him in the garden. But that's enough for tonight – it's your bedtime.'

⌣

Saturday morning was a good time for Li Ping and Little Li to collect horse manure from the stables. Most horses were out working with the men, so only those in foal or recovering from hard rides were in their stalls. And, occasionally, there was a young mare being prepared for covering by the stallion in the mating box. That happened one Saturday in early spring when, as they approached the barn, a now adolescent Little Li ran ahead and came to a sudden stop at the open doorway when she saw the mating horses heaving and snorting.

Li Ping caught up with her and, concerned at this scene, said, 'Come away, Daughter. We'll return later.'

Little Li did not move. She was transfixed and remained staring into the stable after Li Ping reached her. They stood together, watching the exhausted stallion and mare, standing flank to flank, heads down.

The stable hand, a young sandy-haired youth with a wispy beard, asked them to come in and help muck out the stables. Li Ping knew that the moment had come to talk to her daughter about her father. And about herself. She was relieved to feel prepared to tell her daughter anything she wanted to know. Perhaps more.

Li Ping tied a full bag of fresh manure and hay on each end of her old bamboo pole and watched as Little Li did the same. They set off together at a trot toward their newly turned-over vegetable beds. With the smell of leather and hay still in her nostrils, Li Ping felt a thrill at the prospect of telling her daughter how Ah Joe and his horse Music once moved through the Woolshed Valley. Remembering him riding proud and upright showing off his Chinese clothes, she trembled as she recalled them at full gallop – Ah Joe riding hands and heels, the brim of his hat pushed back in the wind, his face almost touching Music's neck.

'Slow down, Mother. You're galloping like a horse. I can't keep up.'

Li Ping slowed.

'I'm hungry', said Little Li.

'Me too. I'll make noodles tonight.'

≈

Little Li leaned forward, her elbows on the scrubbed kitchen table, her chin in her hands as she watched her mother's tiny, wiry fingers interleaving the dough, flicking and stretching it. She coaxed strands of noodles to appear from a pillow of flour and water while their largest cast iron pot boiled away vigorously.

'Please help chop the vegetables. All of them. We've worked very hard today.'

Onions, carrots, turnips with purple tops, cabbage and potatoes and coriander and barley by the handful all went in. The steam, the smells, the lick of flames around the firebox door, the dimming light, the golden lamp wick, and her mother cooking in her flour-dusted tunic delighted Little Li nearly as much as the prospect of her favourite meal.

They ate on the floor without speaking but not in silence. Both slurped and sucked the noodles, filling their mouths with the silky fat worms, as Little Li had called them when she was younger. They chewed the root vegetables and then finished the broth by raising the bowls directly to their lips.

They then set their bowls aside, placed their chopsticks across the brim and looked toward the altar for Guanyin.

'Little Li, it's time for me to tell you how you came to be here. Today we saw the mare and the stallion together making another horse, a baby horse. They're called foals. The one that was made today will grow to become like its mother and its father in ways that we don't yet know. Perhaps it will be mostly grey like its mother? Perhaps it will have long legs like its father? Perhaps it will have a strong will, no matter whether it's male or female? There are many unknowns. But we do know that it is both its mother and its father in a new form.'

'It's the same for all animals and birds and fish. Even bees and flies, I think. You've seen this happening here every year of your life when you saw new chickens and sheep arriving and growing up.'

'People are the same. A female and a male must join. The male gives the seed and the female provides the place for growth.'

'You, my dear, come from an Irishman's seed which was looked after carefully in me. You grew in my body – me, a female from the distant country that Europeans call China – the place of my birth – the Celestial Kingdom.'

'What was the Irishman like, Mother?'

'As I told you before, his name was Ah Joe. His full name was Joe Byrne.'

'Many years ago, I met an old man at a temple who knew Ah Joe well. He told me Ah Joe had more good and more bad in him than most men. The old man was correct.'

'Ah Joe was a playful, clever man who loved writing songs and listening to music. As I told you, he called his horse Music and it was thrilling to see them together. His musical ear allowed him to learn our language very well. He's still the only European I've met who could speak it well enough to have a proper conversation.'

Little Li interrupted her mother, 'Is that why …'

Li Ping continued. 'But he was also a violent man and very dangerous, particularly to his friends if they betrayed him. He shot and killed his best friend before he came to visit me on the last night I ever saw him. It was the night that we joined to make you.'

'Mother – did he force you?'

'No, he did not. That night was like no other moment in my life. I've rarely had strong physical urges of any kind. But, when I did, it was always when someone close to me revealed their heart. No one's ever revealed their heart so fully and so desperately as Ah Joe on that night.'

'All emotions contain pain. I could not stop myself wanting him. No consequences, not even the possibility of you, occurred to me. Nothing was known to me except his grief. Perhaps that's why I've only made love to a man once? Perhaps that's why I've never sought a lover? My deepest feeling for another is aroused by their grief.'

Li Ping paused for some time before continuing.

'Yet, my attention and feeling did so little for him. His anger about killing his best friend returned quickly and he ran to his beautiful Music and galloped away to Glenrowan to join Ned Kelly. They planned to commit an awful atrocity which would have been even worse if they had not been thwarted by their own foolishness. My brother, Li Chen, your uncle, was with him.'

'I know you've heard of the Kelly gang and their killings and robberies. People have been talking about them for years. Yes, your father was a member of that gang – and your uncle was one of their greatest supporters.'

'Within twenty-four hours of leaving me, Ah Joe was shot dead by police and my brother's fragile mind was destroyed by the same violence. He never spoke again.'

'Why did they do these terrible things, Mother?'

'I don't have the full answer, but the sort of liberation that your father, my brother and the Kelly gang wanted could only be gained if they were prepared to kill. The same is true for the men in power who sought to control them', she said, overcome by disturbing recollections.

'The same is also true for your grandfather, Li Wencui. Many years after I left the Celestial Kingdom, a new arrival from our district carried a message from my mother that your grandfather found the courage to join the rebellion against the Qing Dynasty. He was executed by his own people for his views.'

'And my grandmother?'

'I have never heard anything about her life or her death after we repaid our debt to them. I'm sure she would have continued her work with herbs and medicines. I'm certain she remained in the presence of Guanyin and the monastics.'

'I understand travel between this colony and the Celestial Kingdom is much quicker and safer these days. There are now steam ships as well as steam trains.'

'I would like you to make that voyage one day. You'll always have more than one home.'

Little Li was enlivened.

'And are there steamships to Ireland?'

'Perhaps, I'm not sure.'

'And was there killing and rebellion in Ireland?'

'My Daughter, I'm tired now, we can talk again soon. But your question is important. Let's now both go to sleep remembering what the old man at the temple said. "Good and bad" exist within us all, including you and me. And within you runs the blood of rebellion from the north, south, east and west. Tomorrow we'll choose again which seeds to water.'

'Goodnight, Daughter.'

'Goodnight, Mother.'

∽

In the following years, Li Ping and her child always entered the big house together, staying within arm's reach of one another. One ageing and becoming smaller, one growing with no predictable form or a future clear to anyone.

However, one night, for the first time, Little Li entered the big house alone to help serve food for a family dinner. During the meal, the talking was continuous and overlapping with the family making plans to clear more land, buy more stock and bring in Chinese farm labourers.

The red-faced old patriarch, Daman Donnally, thumped the table.

'More Celestials, that's what we need', he said, 'They know how to take orders and be quiet about it. No one else wants them anyway. And no more Catholics, especially Irish Catholics who would rather fight than earn a shilling. Dumb thugs, the lot of them, just like Kelly's gang. Hang 'em all, I say.'

'Let's drink to that', said the eldest son, Gerald, as he raised his glass across the table to give the toast. 'Hang the Irish – here's to the Chinamen.' A loud hurrah followed.

The old man turned in his chair, looking to his servant and pointed at their glasses. Li Ping's child, Little Li, moved self-consciously between the hunched and hungry diners to serve them. The sons of the house now sat motionless during the last of these wine-fuelled monologues waiting for their mother to take up a position which, everyone knew, would be the final word on the matter.

Brenna Donnally took a full draught of her red wine

and put the empty glass down in front of her. She looked past her husband and her sons to the china cabinet in the corner of the dining room – her unsteady, wine-fogged gaze caught the vase that her cousin had returned all those years ago.

She thought of her disguised Catholicism, her greedy love of Chinese treasures, and her longing for true friendship with her now deceased cousin. She also felt her deep unease at being responsible for the half-caste child of a dead Catholic outlaw. Sadness and hopelessness were arising in her.

'We will do as father says', blurted the Galway girl in Brenna Donnally.

～

Li Ping and Little Li had heard these dinner conversations many times before and they were always saddened by them. However, on this occasion, Little Li, now sixteen, felt overwhelming anger. Perhaps because the old man's face became more and more volcanic with each mouthful of meat and wine? Perhaps because his sons and his wife became more like him with every drink? Perhaps because Li Ping was not with her? Whatever the reason or trigger, her youthful chest shuddered.

Anger arising from abuse of parents, their parents and all who went before them, burns hot through everyone and that angry fire coursed through Little Li's veins that night. Memories of being ridiculed by the sons and their housemates for eating with two sticks enraged her, as did the punishment she received years ago for speaking her mother's tongue too loudly.

But people being served by servants may often enjoy a degree of affection, even an expression of love, for those depending on them. This matriarch of the pastoral world, Brenna Donnally, adored Li Ping as her 'little doll'. She meant it sincerely, but Little Li, the child of her little doll, was another matter.

The night had been rowdy and the drinking heavy. Mrs Donnally, very aware of Li Ping's absence when leaving the table, said, 'Little Li, I hope your mother's comfortable'.

~

Earlier that day, Li Ping had slipped into unconsciousness. She lay still in bed. She had not eaten for some days and instructed that under no circumstances should the doctor be called.

While Little Li cleared the table in the big dining room, still angry about the invisibility of the true hearts of all who had made her, her mother's lips were forming words for the final time:

Gaté gaté pāragate pārasamgate bodhi svāhā
Gone, gone, gone beyond, gone fully beyond,
Awakened now!

Li Ping waited for her child to return while her shallow breath, once a warm fabric, a cloth to her child's cheek, was now a mere thread, opening and closing her lungs and her consciousness. In her left hand, she held a tightly rolled scroll of paper resting in the crease of the heart line of her upturned palm.

On entering Li Ping's room, her barefooted child bowed to Guanyin on the bedside shrine. After three breaths, each fully absorbed and then gently expelled toward the old woman, Li Ping's child knelt beside her, taking her mother's left hand in her right hand, cupping the little scroll between them. There they stayed – held in the gaze of Guanyin – held by their joined palms as if they were a single being preparing to bow until Li Ping's last thread of breath parted with a snap, like the cracking of an egg.

The child of two worlds, Li Ping's child, had been fastidiously prepared for what was unfolding. In the immediate moment of the parting of the breath thread, the circulation of joy that Li Ping said should be detected, passed between mother and child, not once but many times as Li Ping commenced the unknowable passage common to us all.

'Tears can be, or they may not be. They are not important. What is important is that you feel my inevitable continuation within you. And the continuation of your father. That, my child, is my joy. One that is yours too, I believe.'

During their discussions about death and funeral arrangements over previous months and years, one thing became very clear to Li Ping. She would not be buried in the manner of the traditions followed in her first home. It took many visits to the temple over many years to accept this truth. Guided by the chanting of the Heart Sutra and the recognition of love arising from Not-Even-Anything-Land, she was able to let go of so much.

However, two matters remained but not as unresolved agonies. They remained as a means of transmission to the one she had breast-fed so many years ago.

Her first concern was for her body not to be shifted for four days. As she was taught as a child in the nunnery, during this time she would commence leaving the body. She told Little Li, 'Consciousness does not disappear when the conscious ones think that death has happened. Please do your best to give me the time needed, my child.'

'At the end of the fourth day, the body will be of no further use to me and should be cremated if Mrs Donnally and her family agree. Otherwise, just bury me in the shroud I've already made. It's in the white box beneath my bed. Which brings me to the second matter. I want you to conduct my cremation, my funeral and the observances on the seventh and the forty-ninth days following my transition. My great wish is that no one else do this for me. I'll leave you a scroll containing instructions to make your passage into the next stage of your life at the same time.'

'And finally, please make sure everyone on this property knows that they're welcome to be with us as we accomplish this together.'

The joy happened as Li Ping said it should. Her child's tears seeped into the grey knitted blanket and disappeared. She lifted the little scroll from Li Ping's palm and spread it out on the floor in front of the lamp-lit shrine.

Li Ping's final words read,

> *Our life together is not over. Look at your right hand. It is me. Look at your left hand, there you'll find Ah Joe. Like me, you have not been male or female to the world around you through your first decade and a half. I am so grateful you've been safe with me in this way for those early years of your life. Of course, I've noticed that Mrs Donnally is uncomfortable now your Irish ancestry is more obvious. And I've noticed the boys and the girls of your age on this property keep a distance from you. Men have shown no interest either in ways that might have been dangerous.*
>
> *But now the great source of continuous change requests a new response from us both. Mine is simple and easy; it is welcome submission. Yours, my child, must be the release for you to choose how to nurture your emergence into womanhood. I cannot tell you the way, but I'm sure that by conducting these arrangements for me, the teachings at the heart of my life will carry you into the wider world correctly.*

The instructions on Li Ping's scroll continued, 'You have been known simply as Little Li all these years. But now, as you look after my progression, I'd like you to accept *Chenmo de zhenai* 沉默的真愛, True Love of Silence. As your mother, I know that coming to be more and more in love with silence is both your protection and your sound continuation in the world of objects.'

⌣

Little Li, now Chenmo, scanned the rest of the scroll. It was, as she thought, the order of service for Li Ping's funeral and the prayer cycle for the seventh and the forty-ninth days. She bent forward from her kneeling position until her forehead touched the smooth, dark earth floor. And, as her mother had done so many times, she unfolded her body until flat to the earth. Her breathing raised and lowered her slim frame like a wavelet on a rising tide. Then, with movements identical to Li Ping's, she began to fold and unfold like a fan. She completed three prostrations to Guanyin.

It took Chenmo more than three hours to wash her mother with warm water and then sprinkle her tiny, smooth body with talcum powder. She showed meticulous devotion to every contact with the form of Li Ping – every beautiful expanse of skin, like her inner forearms and her upturned wrists, every tuck of the body frame, between her knuckles, and down into the softness between her fingers. Silent tears watered

Chenmo's cheeks as she moved her mother's hair aside and wiped her neck below her ear. She dressed her in a white *cheongsam qipao* which Li Ping had made for herself over the hot summer months earlier in the year and laid her back in her bed.

For many hours until dawn, they lay together, mother in some unknowable transition and daughter asleep without dreaming.

～

Chenmo rose as the fog rolled up the valley and over the roof of the big house, masking the steep boulder hills to the east where two wedge-tailed eagles presided. They won't be seen this morning, Chenmo thought as she walked the stone path from the cottage to the big house for the second time alone. She knew that Mrs Donnally would be sitting on her stool beside the fire in the scullery, drinking her first cup of her imported Robur tea.

And there she sat just as Chenmo expected. One kitchen maid was working the large churn, the other peeling apples. Neither turned from their tasks but Mrs Donnally was startled as Chenmo articulated with such surprising directness and clarity what had to be done.

'My mother, Li Ping, has died. She thanks you for your assistance over many years and makes two requests. First, she requests that she may be able to lie in her bed without moving for four days while I maintain a vigil beside her. This is our custom.'

'Of course', replied Mrs Donnally, so alert to the moment, it surprised Chenmo. She seemed somehow embarrassed and weakened.

'And her second request?'

'She wishes to be cremated in the boulder hills on the flat rock overlooking the valley and her last home in *Tsin Chin Shan*. My task is to make all the arrangements, if you give your approval. My mother wanted you and your family and everyone here on the run to know that you can all feel free to attend if you wish.'

'I'll have to talk to the family about this, Little Li', Mrs Donnally said, 'but can I visit Li Ping now?'

Chenmo led the way out of the scullery. Walking through the big house toward the back door, she thought about telling Mrs Donnally her correct name, but now was not a proper time.

It was only a few steps between the back fence of the house garden of the homestead and the front door of the cottage and its wood pile. As the two women crossed this narrow path, Chenmo said, 'Thank you for coming to see Li Ping. She'll be very happy if we can be very quiet while we're with her.' Mrs Donnally nodded, stifling a gasp or a shudder.

Entering Li Ping's bedroom, Chenmo saw her deceased mother in angled early daylight for the first time and thought she looked beautiful. So white and clear. So still.

But Mrs Donnally, ever the matriarch, was struggling now that the ornamental presence of Li Ping had gone.

'You can touch her if you like. Would you like me to leave?'

Mrs Donnally shook her head but walked forward to put her fingertips on Li Ping's shoulder for a moment, then turned and walked slowly back to the big house, her eyes fixed on the ground just ahead of her feet.

⌣

The fog cleared late in the morning, much later than usual, as a brilliant day began in the valley. Wedge-tailed eagles played in the spiral currents of the warming air. Chenmo observed them with delight as she spent her first day of mourning going from the bedside to a sunny spot under the veranda of their cottage and back again.

Just before nightfall, Mrs Donnally returned to say that the family had agreed to the cremation.

'The men will help you with the wood and the transportation of Li Ping.'

'Thank you', Chenmo replied. 'My mother and I thank you. I'll take the wood up over the next three days. I'll enjoy that but I would be very grateful for help to move my mother.'

'Of course', said Brenna Donnally, allowing some tears to fall unchecked, touched by both the gravity and the elegance of Chenmo's address.

'And ma'am, I must tell you, my name now is Chenmo de Zhenai. It means 'True Love of Silence'. You can call me Chenmo if you wish, but Little Li is also correct. Thank you again for helping us.'

Flat Rock was perhaps a mile away to the east across deeply pastured paddocks and then a fifteen-minute steep walk up a well-worn track between the boulders. In the late morning of the second day, Chenmo made her first trip with a barrow of wood to the base of the hill and then carried its contents in four trips up the track and out on to the large overhanging stone. After each trip, she looked up for the wedge-tails and then down into the valley where she could see the vast roof of the big house and, next to it, the little rectangular box where her mother lay. It pleased her that her mother had the time she needed.

She was also happy with her progress with the firewood and loved the neat crisscross pattern of small logs she had built. She felt sure that she could complete the task with one more trip in the afternoon and two trips on the third day and fourth days. Her mind then turned to the fifth day – the day for the cremation, funeral prayers and observances. She thought about who might come. She imagined herself standing beside the burning pyre and wondered how close she would be able to be to her mother.

And below, under the veranda of the big house, Mrs Donnally sat in an old wicker chair and watched Chenmo's every step across the pastures and up the path between the boulders. It seemed that her every movement was somehow measured, utterly regulated, a pattern of motion and effort that might have been controlled from elsewhere.

~

In the little cottage, day two established the order of things for days three and four. Sleep without dreaming, first-light prostrations to Guanyin, washing and powdering Li Ping, first chant of the Heart Sutra, first wood carrying, lunch of rice and radishes, second wood carrying, second chanting and then the absorption of evening into night: sometimes sitting looking westward under the little porch, sometimes on the floor before Guanyin and her mother.

Chenmo reached for her mother's diary and read her final entry.

> *After all these years in Tsin Chin Shan, with the heavens and seasons reversed, I wonder. Do I see reality, or do I see a mirror? But I smile now as I recall Sister Abbess from all those years ago saying, 'we are the mirror itself'.*

On the morning of the fifth day, Chenmo purposefully slipped gently from the shared bed to kneel in front of Guanyin without prostrating. Looking into the man-woman, woman-man face, she reached forward, picked up Guanyin and placed the hand-crafted white jade formation deep into the pocket of her tunic.

Looking out the window with its four-square panes, she realised that she had slept deep into daylight. Soon, the workmen would arrive. She drew back the blanket covering Li Ping, opened the box beside the bed and lifted out the white shroud that her mother had made while noticing that the stitching was identical to her own tunic. Slowly, fold by fold, she slipped Li Ping inside her covering. She untucked the bottom sheet – its four corners hanging loosely just above the floor.

Outside, under the porch, Chenmo positioned the old wooden wheelbarrow to the left of the doorway and waited. She could hear the men approaching from the house garden. As they opened the gate and began to cross the path toward her, they slowed and fell silent. She could see their awkwardness as they came closer, and she smiled toward them.

'Thank you for coming to help us', she said.

The youngest among them, a youth not much older than herself and dressed in what she had observed over the years as 'Sunday clothes', put his hands in his pockets and lowered his head, saying, 'Happy to, ma'am'.

In the one-room cottage, the four men seemed enormous. The proportions of everything changed – what had been regular became tiny, especially Li Ping. There were men's boots on the floor for the first time since the unmarried Chinese mother had moved in and, as they lifted the sheet by its four corners, Li Ping sank deep into the centre of the cloth. Chenmo thought that she looked just like the scroll she had held in her hand five days ago.

A southerly breeze was building as they crossed the pastures, Chenmo wheeling the barrow, two men beside her at a distance and two men just ahead. At the base of the hill, Chenmo untucked the sheet again and the men moved forward, taking a corner each in their big, rough hands and walking up the hill with the mourning daughter ahead of them. Her pace was slow and smooth, and it took some minutes before the men found her rhythm for the climb.

Emerging on to the great overhanging stone, Chenmo was exhilarated by the southerly flow of sharp, cool air.

She felt her lungs sucking, her heart rising and beating strongly after the climb. Slowly the men placed Li Ping on her pyre and Chenmo tucked the sheet under the tiny bundle. One by one, the men went to the pile of eucalyptus branches and placed them on the pyre as directed. They finished their tasks by arranging the final layers of split logs.

Chenmo almost startled herself when saying 'thank you', such was the silence unbroken by a voice since the men had entered the cottage.

'That's all I need for now. Thank you.'

The men shifted awkwardly and the young one said, 'Can we stay?'

'Yes – of course', Chenmo replied. 'We would like that.'

The men backed away toward the hill and sat on a small grassy patch beside the path. Chenmo followed and walked past them. From behind a wiry little wattle forcing its way up between the rocks, Chenmo picked up a flagon of kerosene. Feeling her heartbeat strongly as she walked back to the pyre, she began to chant '*Gaté gaté pāragate pārasamgate bodhi svāhā*'.

To the north, at the head of the pyre, perhaps three yards back, she withdrew Guanyin from her tunic and placed the bodhisattva of compassion on the ground. She knelt as she and her mother had always done and commenced her prostrations, folding and unfolding herself in the fresh breeze as daughter and mother, woman and man, Irish and Chinese, porous to the heart.

And then, as she rose from the final prostration, she looked to the west, down and across to the big house and there, halfway between the hill and the homestead, was Mrs Donnally, without her husband but with her sons, walking in single file toward her and holding outstretched in front of her the vase – the gift that had marked the birth of Joe Byrne.

Chenmo lit the pyre. It roared in the southerly wind, carrying embers over the green pastures and over the family below who were walking resolutely toward her. Chenmo was deeply moved by knowing that, when the flames died, she would lead the prayers her mother had selected, in the presence of the people who had given them both a home all those years ago.

Timeline of Historic Events

1840 First references to Chinese people as 'the Celestials' start to appear in Victorian newspapers. [Trove]

1850 The Taiping Rebellion against the Qing Dynasty begins in southern China and rages for fourteen years, killing tens of millions, led by Hong Xuiquan, a self-proclaimed brother of Jesus Christ. [*Encyclopaedia Britannica*]

1853 First Chinese gold-seekers arrive in Victoria. [Museums of History, New South Wales]

1854 or 1855 Edward (Ned) Kelly is born at Beveridge, Victoria, the eldest son of John ('Red') Kelly and his wife Ellen (née Quinn). [*Australian Dictionary of Biography*, Australian National University]

1855 Government of Victoria imposes a tax on all Chinese citizens entering Victoria. Ship's masters required to pay a tax of £10 for every Chinese on board. All Chinese entering required to register and live within designated areas and pay a resident tax of £1 per annum. [Old Treasury Building Museum Archives]

1856–60   Britain wages the Second Opium War against China to maintain its opium trade, against the wishes of Chinese governments. [*Encyclopaedia Britannica*]

1856   November, Joe Byrne born in the Woolshed Valley near Beechworth to Paddy Byrne and his wife Margaret (née White). The family property is next to the Chinese camp. [*The Friendship That Destroyed Ned Kelly*, Ian Jones]

1857   Chinese immigration to *Tsin Chin Shan*, 'New Gold Mountain' (Victoria): 25,424 of 456,522 or 5.6% of the population rising to 8.2% in 1859 [Benjamin Mountford, 'In Search of Fook Shing', Honours Thesis, University of Melbourne, 2007, Appendix 1]

1857   The Bombardment of Guangzhou by the British Navy [*Encyclopaedia Britannica*]

1857   Buckland River riots. Two thousand Chinese driven from the Buckland Valley goldfields by a European mob. Three Chinese killed, camps and temple destroyed. Thirteen Europeans arrested; all acquitted to the cheers of the crowd at the court. ['The Trial of the Buckland River Rioters', *Argus*, 12 August 1857]

1857   European miners form an Anti-Chinese League in Beechworth to raise funds to defend the Buckland River rioters. [*Ovens Murray Advertiser*, 8 August 1857]

1857   Sailing vessel the *Land O'Cakes* arrives in Robe, South Australia, to avoid the Victorian tax. Two

	hundred and sixty-four Chinese passengers are rowed ashore and commence the walk to the Victorian goldfields. [Monumentaustralia.org.au]
1857–63	Sixteen and a half thousand Chinese men and one woman are landed in Robe and head for the Victorian goldfields. [Monumentaustralia.org.au]
1858	Chinese population of Australia reaches peak of forty thousand, representing 3.3% of the total population. This number is not reached again until the late 1980s. [National Archives of Australia]
1860–61	Lambing Flat riots. Up to three thousand Europeans attack two thousand Chinese and drive them off the diggings. [*Encyclopaedia Britannica*]
1869	Ned Kelly arrested for the robbery and assault of Chinese man Ah Fook but found 'not guilty' because of three corroborating witness statement accounts for Kelly and none for Ah Fook. [*The Ned Kelly Encyclopaedia*, Justin Corfield]
1870s	Joe Byrne and his mother live on family dairy farm on the boundary of the Chinese camp in the Woolshed Valley, just out of Beechworth. [*The Friendship That Destroyed Ned Kelly*, Ian Jones]
1870s	Joe Byrne becomes fluent in Chinese and smokes opium. [*The Friendship That Destroyed Ned Kelly*, Ian Jones]
1870s	Margaret Byrne develops 'intimate friendships' with the Chinese, according to evidence given at the 1881 Royal Commission into the Police of Victoria.

1878	Stringybark Creek gunfight – three police shot and killed by the Kelly gang. [*The Ned Kelly Encyclopaedia*, Justin Corfield]
1878	Friday 15 November, the Kelly gang declared outlaws – police or civilians permitted to shoot gang members on sight. [*The Friendship That Destroyed Ned Kelly*, Ian Jones]
1879	7 November, Kelly and Byrne travel to Jerilderie and write the Jerilderie letter with the intention of having it printed. However, the publisher of the *Jerilderie Gazette* runs away and the letter is handed to police in 1880 by the Jerilderie Bank accountant. The letter warns authorities of impending rebellion if injustices inflicted by the colonial government of Victoria do not cease. [*The Ned Kelly Encyclopaedia*, Justin Corfield]
1879	14 March, Kelly writes to the Premier of New South Wales, 'Now Sir Henry I tell you that highway robbery is only in its infancy for the white population is been driven out of the labour market by an inundation of Mongolians and when the white man is driven to desperation there will be desperate times.' [IronOutlaw.com and *Ned Kelly: After a Century of Acrimony*, John Meredith and Bill Scott]
1879	Colonial authorities start detaining suspected Kelly sympathisers for up to three months without trial. [*The Ned Kelly Encyclopaedia*, Justin Corfield]

1880	Chinese community supports Kelly gang with supplies from Chinese stores. [Royal Commission Minute 1477]
1880	Chinese Detective Fook Shing is sent to northeast Victoria to investigate rumours that the Kelly gang was being harboured, supplied and supported by the Chinese community of the district. [Benjamin Mountford, 'In Search of Fook Shing', Honours Thesis, University of Melbourne, 2007]
1880	'Wanted' posters and leaflets in Cantonese distributed in northeast Victoria. [Royal Commission Minute 5846 and *The Ned Kelly Encyclopaedia*, Justin Corfield]
1880	Siege of Glenrowan. Skyrocket fireworks launched by supporters of Kelly in the bush behind the Glenrowan Hotel. [*The Friendship That Destroyed Ned Kelly*, Ian Jones]
1880	Kelly arrested and taken to Melbourne Gaol.
1880	On his way to Melbourne while under arrest, Kelly tells his accompanying police officer, Mounted Constable Alfred John Faulkner, 'If I could grow a tail (that is, a Chinaman's tail) I would go home to China, as one China-man was worth all (expletive deleted) Europeans, and I would rather trust my life to any of them than any (expletive deleted) European living'. Kelly's remarks to Faulkner are recorded as evidence to the 1881 Royal Commission into the Police of Victoria. [Royal Commission evidence, 5488, 11/5/1881]

1880	Kelly found guilty. On 7 November, more than 30,000 signatures are included in a petition stating, 'Your humble petitioners respectfully pray that the Life of the CONDEMNED man, EDWARD KELLY, may be spared'. It is presented on the steps of the Victorian Parliament. Many signatures are duplicated. On 8 November, request denied. [Public Record Office Victoria]
1880	11 November, Kelly hanged.
1930	Authorities release full contents of the Jerilderie letter for the first time. (For speculation by the late Chief Justice of Victoria, John Harber Phillips AC QC, in 2003, that the letter was kept secret until after Kelly's execution for fear of civil unrest given the rousing nature of the text, see below at 2003.)
1980	*Age* journalist and theatre critic, the late Leonard Radic, finds a handwritten note declaring the formation of a republic in northeast Victoria in a regional museum in the United Kingdom. The document was said to be written by Kelly and Byrne. However, Radic was never able to locate the object again. [*The Ned Kelly Encyclopaedia*, Justin Corfield]
2002	9 March 2002, eminent Kelly scholar, Ian Jones, is interviewed by Ben Collins and the transcript is published in the Ironoutlaw.com. 'What things did you leave out of your books that you would have liked to share with your readers?' He replied, 'An omission from my biography of Ned, which I would like to rectify in a revised

edition sometime, was the role of the Chinese which I wish I had given proper emphasis. The Chinese played a very significant part in the Kelly story. Ned had great respect for the Chinese and Joe, of course, was virtually a member of Beechworth's Chinese community.'

2003   Former Chief Justice of Victoria, the late John Harber Phillips AC QC, speculates in the inaugural Kerford Lecture in Beechworth that the full contents of the Jerilderie letter was kept secret by authorities until after Kelly's execution for fear of civil unrest given the rousing nature of the text, which includes: 'It will pay the government to give those people who are suffering innocence, justice and liberty, if not, I will be compelled to show some colonial stratagem which will open the eyes of not only the Victoria Police, but also the whole British Army'. [The Inaugural G.B. Kerford Oration, 'The North-East Victoria Republic Movement – Myth or Reality', The Hon. John Harber Phillips AC, Chief Justice of Victoria. La Trobe University Media Releases 2003, 'Chief Justice to Give 2003 Telstra La Trobe University George Briscoe Kerford Oration']

The Heart Sutra

Buddhists all over the world have been chanting, reading, studying and translating the Heart Sutra since mid-600 CE. My exposure to and engagement with the cryptic text has been through the Zen traditions of Japan and Vietnam.

Vietnamese Zen monk, the late Thich Nhat Hanh (1929–2022), has been my teacher over two decades. For a profound and accessible commentary, I recommend his book *The Heart of Understanding: Commentaries on the Prajnaparamita Heart Sutra*, published by Parallax Press, Berkeley, California.

My personal responses to the ancient text are expressed in *The Celestials* through the principal character Li Ping and her monastic teachers. Li Ping is a fictional character drawn, in significant part, from my periods of living and practising with monks and nuns of Thich Nhat Hanh's order, the Order of Interbeing. The 'clue' to the sutra, I believe, is found in the name of the Zen Master's order, 'Interbeing' – meaning that nothing stands alone and the depth of that realisation has a marked effect on the lives we live.

In this short note, I provide the reader with the 2017 translation by Thich Nhat Hanh. I also provide some words of my own which follow the form of many translations. My words should not be thought of as a translation, but rather a personal response at the time of writing *The Celestials*.

I only have one suggestion if you feel inclined to make your own exploration of the Heart Sutra: observe your responses in a kindly way, whatever they may be.

Ian David Roberts 2023

The Heart Sutra
The Insight That Brings Us to the Other Shore
By Thich Nhat Hanh

Avalokiteshvara,
while practicing deeply with
the Insight that Brings Us to the Other Shore,
suddenly discovered that
all of the five Skandhas are equally empty,
and with this realisation
he overcame all Ill-being.

'Listen Sariputra,
this Body itself is Emptiness
and Emptiness itself is this Body.
This Body is not other than Emptiness
and Emptiness is not other than this Body.
The same is true of Feelings,
Perceptions, Mental Formations,
and Consciousness.

'Listen Sariputra,
all phenomena bear the mark of Emptiness;
their true nature is the nature of
no Birth no Death,
no Being no Non-being,
no Defilement no Purity,
no Increasing no Decreasing.

'That is why in Emptiness,
Body, Feelings, Perceptions,
Mental Formations and Consciousness
are not separate self-entities.

'The Eighteen Realms of Phenomena
which are the six Sense Organs,
the six Sense Objects,
and the six Consciousnesses
are also not separate self-entities.
The Twelve Links of Interdependent Arising
and their Extinction
are also not separate self-entities.
Ill-being, the Causes of Ill-being,
the End of Ill-being, the Path,
insight and attainment,
are also not separate self-entities.

'Whoever can see this
no longer needs anything to attain.

'Bodhisattvas who practice
the Insight that Brings Us to the Other Shore
see no more obstacles in their mind,
and because there
are no more obstacles in their mind,
they can overcome all fear,

destroy all wrong perceptions
and realize Perfect Nirvana.

'All Buddhas in the past, present and future
by practicing
the Insight that Brings Us to the Other Shore
are all capable of attaining
Authentic and Perfect Enlightenment.

'Therefore Sariputra,
it should be known that
the Insight that Brings Us to the Other Shore
is a Great Mantra,
the most illuminating mantra,
the highest mantra,
a mantra beyond compare,
the True Wisdom that has the power
to put an end to all kinds of suffering.
Therefore, let us proclaim
a mantra to praise
the Insight that Brings Us to the Other Shore.

'Gate, Gate, Paragate, Parasamgate, Bodhi Svaha!
Gate, Gate, Paragate, Parasamgate, Bodhi Svaha!
Gate, Gate, Paragate, Parasamgate, Bodhi Svaha!'

(From Thich Nhat Hanh, *The Other Shore*,
Parallax Press, 2017)

The Heart Sutra: The Perfection of Wisdom
A Personal Response by Ian David Roberts

Avalokiteshvara,
who understands body, mind and heart as
inseparable from all things,
flows with compassion for all,
free of anxiety,
knowing that no thing stands alone.

Turning to Shariputra,
the wisest disciple of the Buddha,
Avalokiteshvara says
'Form arises from the infinite cosmos
but the infinite is not separate from form.
The infinite cosmos is not harnessed by form.
and form always returns to the infinite.
The same is true for thoughts and feelings.
No thing stands alone – no eye, no ear, no nose,
no tongue, no body, no mind
and no senses of any kind,
or activity of mind,
All manifest out of the infinite and return to
infinity.

Therefore
Form is within the infinite
and the infinite is within form.
The infinite is the all-encompassing essence,

the truest nature of all –
all that is seen
and felt
and thought.

As the infinite there is no age, no death, no birth.

The eternally generating nature of the infinite is free of suffering,
free of no suffering,
free of cessation of suffering,
free of wisdom
and achievement.

Here we find the unhindered heart mind,
free of fear,
dwelling in the deepest knowing:
awareness beyond wisdom
where equanimity is immeasurable.

All those of the past, present and future
who abide in the full awareness of the eternally generating infinite,
are free of illusion.

Knowing that the realisation of awareness beyond wisdom

is beyond thought,
and beyond the words,
the devoted ones go beyond themselves
by chanting the mantra of unsurpassed breadth
and depth.

gaté gaté paragaté parasamgaté bodhi svaha
gaté gaté paragaté parasamgaté bodhi svaha
gaté gaté paragaté parasamgaté bodhi svaha

(gone, gone, gone beyond (thinking), gone well
beyond (thinking and wisdom), awakened now)

Acknowledgements

With unending thanks to:
Barry Hill
Graham Pitts
Christine Langtree
Jonathan Mills
Dr Zheng Ting, Wang
Annie Lanyon
Richard Mills AM
Harold Mitchell AC
Julie Kantor AO
John Timlin
Snowe Li
Evan Roberts
Phillip Huggins
Bev Roberts (no relation)
Corrie Perkin
Eugenia Flynn
Michael Colgan OBE
Karen Martin
Liz Huggins
Cris Larner
Marg Connors
Jan Wositzky OAM
The Monastic and Lay Sanghas of Nhap Luu
Yufeng Guo

and the generous support of:
Bronte Adams AM
Marilyn Cornally
Wesley Enoch AM
Michael Leighton Jones
Sonia T. Lindsay
Karen Martin
Anza Peart
Robbynne Quiggin
Wendy Sanders
Janet Whiting AM

www.ingramcontent.com/pod-product-compliance
Ingram Content Group UK Ltd.
Pitfield, Milton Keynes, MK11 3LW, UK
UKHW041829140425
457310UK00004B/12